"You'll have to d
or you won't con
you're madly i

He lowered his head toward hers.

She continued to struggle in vain. His lips were mere inches from hers, and one hand remained around her waist, while the other moved to her hair. He released her silky tresses from their confining clasp, allowing the shoulder-length tendrils to slide over his fingers as he pulled her resisting mouth toward his. As he had known it would, her hair felt like silk against his fingers. His appreciative eyes swept her distraught face thoroughly.

"I prefer your hair loose, remember?"

"Mr. Ashton, I don't care what you prefer."

"Oh, but you will care." Her voice caught in her throat at his softly voiced promise. "Call me Derrick."

"No." She strained against his ironclad embrace.

"You'll say my name on moans of passion in just a few seconds."

"Never."

She knew her denial lacked believability because her voice was breathless and a strange feeling began forming in her suddenly churning stomach.

"We'll see."

Before she could acidly respond, determined lips closed over hers in a strong caress.

Books by Judy Lynn Hubbard

Kimani Romance

These Arms of Mine

JUDY LYNN HUBBARD

is a native of Dallas, Texas, and has always been an avid reader—particularly of romance. Judy enjoys well-written, engaging stories with characters she can identify with and root for.

Judy has always loved the craft of writing, and her goal is to touch readers emotionally with her stories. She is thrilled to be releasing her first Kimani Romance novel.

These Arms of MINE

JUDY LYNN HUBBARD

KIMANI
ROMANCE

To my beloved sister, Carol. I wish you were here
to see this day, but you'll live forever in my heart.

KIMANI PRESS™

Recycling programs
for this product may
not exist in your area.

ISBN-13: 978-0-373-86247-4

THESE ARMS OF MINE

Copyright © 2012 by Judy Lynn Hubbard

www.kimanipress.com

Printed in U.S.A.

Dear Reader,

I love it when two destined souls meet and fall in love—even if the road to happily-ever-after is a little rocky. After all, the journey is as important as the destination.

Meet Derrick Ashton, an alpha male who's handsome, sensual, successful—and just a tad vindictive.

Alesha Robinson is beautiful, loyal and selfless and has been given a second chance at happiness, if she can undo the monumental damage her well-intentioned white lies has created.

Soon she'll be a new bride, but can she convince Derrick to give her time to make the transition from his wife on paper to his wife in the bedroom? After all, she is an inexperienced virgin, but he won't believe that—especially since she's given him every reason to think just the opposite is true!

Buckle your seat belts!

Look for my next book, *Our First Dance,* in July 2012.

www.JudyLynnHubbard.com
Twitter: @JudyLynnHubbard
Facebook: Judy Lynn Hubbard

Prologue

Alesha Robinson took a deep breath and held it in for several long seconds before releasing it slowly. She continued the silent argument with herself to combat the foolhardiness of what she was about to do. She should turn around and go home. She started to do it—for the thousandth time, she started to do it—however, she kept walking, almost running toward her destination, as if she were eager for the impending meeting when nothing could be further from the truth.

Would he listen to her? Was there a chance in hell that he would understand and forgive her? Was she just fooling herself by thinking she could appeal to his good side? In the short time they had dated two years earlier, she had often been privy to his charm, wit and good humor. He had been a perfect gentleman, someone she had wanted to get to know better, but circumstances had not worked in their favor. For reasons he still was unaware of, she had abruptly ended their relationship without explanation. Would he hold that against her now?

He had a reputation of being fair and she knew firsthand that he was, or rather had been. But was she remembering a man from a lifetime ago? Did she dare hope that man still existed after the horrible way they had parted?

She mumbled a slight apology after nearly colliding with another pedestrian on the sidewalk, then continued on her way. She was almost there, and still she had no idea what she was going to say to him. She resolved to cross that bridge when she came to it and continued determinedly on her way to an unscheduled yet overdue meeting.

She pulled her light coat tighter around her as a biting blast of October wind forced its unwelcomed way in between the gaps of the coat's loosely tied opening. Absent fingers brushed a stray strand of shoulder-length curly black hair, which had been loosened from its clasp by the teasing gust. What was she going to say? How should she begin? She rehearsed one scenario and then another, and another, yet she still had no idea what would come out of her mouth when she opened it.

Her hesitant feet suddenly stopped outside the forty-story building that was her destination. Craning her head, she glanced up the tall, foreboding black glass frame. She wondered, would the foe she must now face be as formidable and as unyielding? Lowering her eyes to the front door, she took another deep breath and exhaled it before walking through the double doors to face the fire, uncertain she could evade the scorching that was sure to come.

Chapter 1

Derrick Chandler stared in exasperation at the man sitting across from him. Why did campaign managers always have to try to change your life? He listened in annoyance as Cameron Stewart continued to tell him what he must do in order to win the Senate race, which he had recently entered.

He wondered why he hadn't just stuck to corporate law instead of throwing his hat into the political arena. He decided the main reason was the city in which he resided—if you were a successful lawyer and lived in Washington, D.C., it seemed predestined that a foray into the world of politics would occur at some time or another.

Fingers absently tapped his chocolate-colored, clean-shaven chin impatiently and then brushed a piece of lint off the breast pocket of his immaculate navy blue suit. After Cameron talked until he was satisfied, then Derrick would have his say—the other man in the room would not be pleased with what he would hear. He disliked anyone telling him what he should and should not do, and Cam was treading on dangerous ground.

"Derrick, the simple fact is that you need a wife." Cam succinctly summed up his ten-minute tirade.

Derrick bolted upright in his chair, his gray eyes growing hard and cold. His voice matched his angry countenance. "And you need a psychiatrist."

Cam sighed audibly, not in the least put off by his friend's frigid tone. "Just listen to me…"

"No, you listen to me." Derrick held up a hand forestalling his friend's words. "I tried the marriage scene once, and we both know what a fiasco that was."

"Well, I told you before you married her…"

Derrick's darkening eyes stopped Cam cold. "You're treading on dangerous ground, Cameron."

"I know, Derrick, but just hear me out." He quickly continued before his friend could object, "You hired me to increase your chances of being elected and, whether you like it or not, I've got to tell you what I think."

"Well, I don't like it, but if you want to hear yourself talk, be my guest."

He scratched his lightly bearded chin. "We're doing great in all demographics except for women."

Derrick frowned. "I thought our numbers looked pretty good there."

"Pretty good, but if you had a woman in your life, one who could relate with and talk to other women, one on one, about their concerns, I have no doubt our numbers would double."

"Wouldn't a female member of my staff work?"

"Please!" Cam's look of disgust elicited a chuckle. "Man, this is America—the land of opportunity, the home of apple pie and baseball."

Derrick rolled his eyes. "This sure sounds like a commercial."

"With the election a little over a year away, now is the perfect time for you to be seen as someone who has deep ties to the community, someone who has something in common with his constituents, someone who shares their dreams and hopes. The best way to identify with them is to be seen as a family man."

"You're not married."

"I'm not running for public office, either." Cam folded his arms across his chest. "You are and you need someone, and not just any woman—a wife. Just think about it, a built-in hostess for parties and a date ready and willing to go with you whenever and wherever. I know I'm getting through to you." Cam carefully studied Derrick's purposefully unreadable expression.

"Wouldn't a German shepherd accomplish the same thing as a wife?" Derrick smiled slightly.

Cam closed his eyes in frustration before quickly opening them again. "Will you try to see my point of view?"

"No, you try to see mine. I am not going to marry anyone ever again!" He deliberately emphasized each word.

Cam opened his mouth to speak, but closed it again as a buzz sounded from the phone on the desk.

Derrick yanked up the handset impatiently. "Yes, what is it?"

He was more than a little annoyed—he had left instructions not to be disturbed.

"If she won't tell you, then tell her I'm in conference and can't be disturbed!"

He unceremoniously slammed the receiver back into its cradle. He made a mental note to apologize to Dorothy once Cameron left. He was in a foul mood, brought on by the other man's ludicrous suggestion.

Cam was shaking his head disapprovingly. "People skills, Derrick. People skills!"

"What do I pay you for?" In spite of himself, he almost smiled at his friend's dismayed tone.

"To tell you what others dare not."

"Well, you certainly seem to enjoy that part of the job." This time, a genuine smile tilted the corners of his frowning mouth.

"My mother always told me I love a challenge, and you certainly are that." Cam picked up his briefcase and prepared to leave.

"Are we done?"

"Yes, we're done. I'll try to sell you on getting a wife later."

"Oh, joy." Derrick rose to shake his hand.

"Do you have anything else you need to talk to me about?"

"No, please go." Derrick reclaimed his seat behind the desk.

"See you tonight at seven sharp."

As Cam walked toward the door, Derrick grimaced at the thought of another political dinner/debate—he loved the debates, but he detested sitting around with strangers, making senseless small talk over steak or chicken that tasted like rubber and vegetables that had much in common with plastic.

"How could I forget?"

"Just be there, and on time."

"Anything else, Mom?"

"As a matter of fact, yes. But I don't have the strength to discuss it with you right now." He ran a hand over his bald head. "I used to have hair before you and I became friends."

"Later, Cameron." Derrick's sigh turned into a chuckle at

the exasperated look he received before his friend left with a decisive click of the door.

Alone at last, he laughed out loud and ran a hand over his short-cropped hair. He enjoyed needling Cam, almost as much as he enjoyed his newfound career in politics. Best friends since law school, Derrick and Cam looked like brothers—each sharing the same dark coloring, height and build. They had been friendly rivals who had quickly developed a deep, lasting friendship.

Another chuckle escaped from his lips. Cam was right— Derrick could always count on him to say what others dared not to. He supposed that was one of the reasons he liked him so much. That and the fact that he had always been intensely loyal and dependable—two attributes Derrick valued greatly.

Picking up from his desktop a manila folder containing information on his running mate, he reclined in his plush black-leather chair as he began to leaf through the pages carefully, familiarizing himself with every detail—it was always best to know one's opponent better than oneself.

Curious as raised voices wafted through the closed door to his assistant's office, Derrick wondered what had prompted the argument. Seconds later, the door abruptly swung open to admit a woman he thought he would never see again—Alesha Robinson. Automatically, he stood and his icy eyes locked with her uneasy ones.

"It's all right, Dorothy. I'll see Miss Robinson."

He broke eye contact and nodded curtly in his assistant's direction. The woman glanced angrily at Alesha before firmly closing the door as she left.

He felt as if he had been punched hard in the gut, and it wasn't a pleasant feeling. Alesha Robinson was here, standing a few feet away from him, looking as beautiful as he remembered. Damn her! Damn himself for wanting to quickly close the distance between them, crush her in his arms and fuse his starving mouth with hers.

"What brings you to my door, Alesha?" He silently blessed his voice for sounding coolly controlled, when he felt anything but.

She looked lovelier than he remembered, dressed in a plain white sweater and black slacks. That silky light brown skin of hers begged to be caressed. His fingers itched to oblige. Her thick black hair was pulled back from her face, held in a clasp at her nape. He knew from experience that her hair was soft—softer than anything else this world had to offer. To keep from walking over to her he sat back down in his chair. His eyes then went to her left hand and he wasn't sure whether he was relieved or angered that no engagement or wedding ring rested there.

He continued to survey her hungrily. His eyes drank in every aspect of her face, afraid she was a mirage he had to memorize before she quickly disappeared. He had sometimes wondered if the predicament her brother had gotten himself into would force them to see each other again. He couldn't decide if he was glad or angry that outside pressure had precipitated her return to his life, instead of her own desire.

Her steps faltered as her eyes refamiliarized themselves with Derrick's extremely handsome face—she had almost forgotten the effect the mere sight of him had on her. Since their first chance meeting when they had both stopped to help out at the scene of a multicar accident, he had done strange things to her equilibrium. Although currently his face was hard and foreboding, she remembered how his infectious smile could send her heart racing frantically. He sat before her after all this time like a statue—a beautiful bronze statue, she amended. She recalled how unbending his body had been against the yielding softness of hers—they had been the perfect complement for each other in so many ways. That is, until everything had fallen apart by her own hands.

Her stomach churned queasily and her heart began beating faster and louder in her ears as she stopped just in front of the mahogany desk behind which he sat. Her heart leaped in her chest, but was it from anxiety or happiness at seeing him again? Anxiety, definitely. She was here for business—to ask him for a monumental favor—and for no other reason.

"Mr. Chandler, I need to speak with you." She was pleased with the steadiness of her precise and crisply articulated sentence.

"Why so formal, Alesha?"

"I'm here to discuss business, Mr. Chandler."

She made her voice curt, hoping the tone would end his unnerving inspection of her, which was causing every nerve ending in her body to silently cry out for what she knew from experience was his masterful touch.

He had an almost irrepressible desire to trace his fingers down that silky skin of hers—it couldn't possibly be as soft as he remembered. Yet, instinctively, he knew it was. And her full, faintly tinted brown lips—would kissing her still feel like exquisite torture? Pure heaven, that was how he remembered feeling with her in his arms, and he was sure that observation was still accurate.

She waited uneasily for him to say something, anything. He seemed content to just stare at her. Piercing eyes traveled leisurely over her. What was he thinking? Instinctively, she knew she didn't want to know. Was he as disconcerted by seeing her again as she was at seeing him? She couldn't tell—he seemed cold, almost frigid. She felt like fleeing. Why didn't he say or do something?

"Mr. Chandler?"

"I'm busy."

He was annoyed at himself for behaving like a moon-struck idiot. With great effort, he tore his eyes away from her lovely face and angrily picked up a piece of paper from his desk. It took all his self-restraint to totally ignore her.

She bit back the angry retort that sprang to her lips at his callous actions. One thing she didn't need was to put him on the defensive. She had come to him for help, after all—help that she really didn't deserve.

"Surely you can spare me a few moments." Her tone indicated she would accept nothing less.

He returned the paper to his desk and reluctantly looked at her once again. He mentally scolded himself as he felt his pulse rate increase as she ran her tongue over her upper lip.

"What do you want?"

She silently cursed him for asking a question he obviously knew the answer to. *You might offer me a seat first,* she silently fumed.

"I'm here about Robert."

At the mention of her brother's name, he closed the folder in front of him and motioned for her to be seated in the chair Cam had just vacated. She was painfully aware of the intense focus of his eyes and an emotion she dared not name hidden in their now-frigid depths.

"I was wondering when he would send you in to plead his case." In fact, he had been counting on it.

Her spine stiffened in the soft leather chair and quickly contradicted him. "He didn't. I came on my own to ask you not to press charges against him."

He smiled slightly at that. "You must be as mad as your brother is if you think I'm going to allow him to embezzle $100,000 from my campaign fund and just walk away, free as a bird."

"If you will just let me explain…" She squared her shoulders for a fight she had known was inevitable.

"There's no explanation you have that I am interested in hearing. He took the money—that's all I need to know."

"Regardless, I'm going to tell you the reason my brother *borrowed* the money from you."

His eyes narrowed at the slight edge evident in her tone. What did she have to be bent out of shape about? He was the one who had been wronged by her brother—and by her. What right did she have to treat him as the villain or even to be here asking anything of him?

"*Borrowed?* That's an interesting choice of words. Go on. Tell me, why did your brother *borrow* the money?" He crossed his arms across his broad chest, drawing attention to his muscular physique.

She had the feeling she was wasting her time, but she had to try, for her family's sake. Maybe he would be sympathetic once he learned why Robert had stolen from him. At least she prayed he would.

"Well?" he prompted. "Let me guess. He used it to bet on the ponies." At her blank stare he tried again. "The slots? Sports? Cards?"

"I don't approve of my brother's actions."

"Neither do I and I intend to make my disapproval a matter of public record by filing charges against him." When she remained silent, he continued, "I don't know what you hoped to accomplish by coming here." *Except to remind me of what you needlessly snatched away from me—from both of us—two years ago.*

At this moment neither did she. "I thought I could make you understand."

"Did your brother take my money?"

"Yes." The single word was spoken through gritted teeth.

"Was it his money to take?" He continued in the same no-nonsense courtroom tone.

"You know it wasn't!" She felt like a petulant child he was taking great pleasure in chastising.

Yes, Robert had been wrong to take Derrick's money, but couldn't he show a little compassion? She wondered how much of his unbending attitude had more to do with her past actions than with Robert's thievery.

He had been dreaming of and dreading this moment for two long years. Against his will, he noticed those heavenly eyes of hers sparkle as her temper rose, making her even more beautiful, more desirable. His inappropriate observations annoyed him, making his next words clipped and terse.

"By your own admission, and your brother's, he committed a crime—a felony. What more do I need to understand?" He opened the folder on his desk again, dismissing her.

"Robert's sorry."

He laughed without humor. "I'm sure he is, now that he's been caught."

She was favored with another of his piercing gazes. And somehow resisted the almost irrepressible urge to run as fast and as far from him as her legs could carry her. Even after two years, he still unnerved her completely while he seemed completely unaffected by seeing her again. No, that wasn't true. He was angry, but not at her brother.

"He knows what he did was wrong."

"Well, that's very touching, but it doesn't replace my $100,000, does it?"

He was tired of talking about her brother and would much rather talk about her. What had she done in the two years they had been apart? Had she missed him? Had she second-guessed and third-guessed her fateful decision that had ruined both of their lives? Had she spent sleepless nights wondering where he was and whom he was with? He hoped so. Because against his better judgment, he had thought about her often—about the satisfying relationship they could and should have been enjoying during that time, if only she hadn't destroyed things between them.

He was disheartened to learn that despite her betrayal, she still had the power to move him and make him want to rewrite their story to his satisfaction. Why couldn't they turn back the clock and be meeting coincidentally for the first time? Why did they have to be enemies by virtue of their past relationship?

She remembered him as caring, compassionate and passionate. He had made her feel as if she were the most important person in the world to him. He had made her want to lose herself in him. He had both thrilled and frightened her. Where had that Derrick Chandler gone? Had she somehow destroyed him? If she had, why did that thought disturb her so much?

"I have a lot of work to do."

He needed to get her out of here before he made a complete fool of himself. He didn't like where his memories were leading him or how hard he had to fight to keep himself from touching her. She had nearly ruined his life, and he shouldn't want anything to do with her, should he?

"We'll pay you back."

He sighed fully before giving her his full attention again. "When?"

"As soon as we can." At his dubious look she nearly shouted, "You don't need the money. You don't even miss it!"

"That's not the point."

The coldest eyes she had ever encountered locked on hers. She forced herself not to retreat from his frigid gaze—she knew from past experience he could utterly melt a woman's heart and resistance without even trying. After all this time, he still unnerved her. He made her feel completely raw and vulnerable.

"So, what is the point?"

"Your brother took something that belonged to me. No one does that without suffering the consequences—no one."

The darkening of her eyes let him know that his reference to their relationship was not lost on her.

"How can you be so heartless?"

"Look, I didn't ask your brother to embezzle funds from me, and I didn't ask you to come here today, pleading with me to show mercy to someone who should be—no, who will be—prosecuted."

Why didn't she leave and stop torturing him with her very presence? Lord, what had he done in his life to deserve this?

"I don't know what else to say." She closed her eyes as if seeking divine intervention.

Unable to bear staring at her beauty another second, he swiveled his chair to look out the huge wall-to-wall windows. "You can show yourself out."

She quickly weighed telling him the real reason Robert had embezzled from him. It had nothing to do with gambling, as he had suggested. If he knew Robert's actions were motivated out of love, not greed, would it change his attitude? Would the truth soften his hard heart? She didn't want to bare her soul to him, but if it would save her brother, she didn't have a choice in the matter.

"Won't you please just listen to me?" She faced the back of his head. "Robert's not what you think. He took the money because…"

He swiveled in his chair and held up a hand to forestall the remainder of her explanation. He'd had enough and needed her to leave.

"Alesha, I don't care why Robert took the money—all that matters is that he's an embezzler! Nothing you have to say will change that or make me change my mind about pressing charges against him. I've heard you out, now goodbye."

She quickly stood, realizing she was wasting her time. There was no use in trying to appeal to his better nature. His words made that perfectly clear and she had no intention of giving him the satisfaction of watching her beg.

She snatched up her purse. "What happened to you? How did you become so cold?"

"I am what people like you have made me."

God, she was torturing him. Her very presence tormented him; yet she also made him feel like he hadn't felt in a long, long time, and he was angry and unsettled by that.

"You are what you want to be." She was angry with herself and with her absurd reaction to seeing him again. "I'm sorry I wasted your time." She turned and walked toward the door.

"Alesha?"

He spoke her name softly, almost caressingly. She felt it run down her spine like soothing, exciting fingers of desire—the sensation stopped her in her tracks. She prayed he would stop being so informal with her because the way he said her name—intimately, for her alone—was destroying her. How could a man's voice stroke her in forbidden places so forcefully that she wanted nothing more than to be utterly immersed in him?

She was about to walk out. However, despite his better judgment, he didn't want her to go. What was it about Alesha Robinson that had always sent his blood simmering and then, just as quickly, boiling out of control?

She turned turbulent eyes on him. "We don't have anything else to say to each other."

"You started this, Alesha." He arrogantly lifted an eyebrow before deliberately adding, "And I'm going to finish it."

"We're done."

She turned to leave again, not just because he annoyed

and angered her, but because there was something about Derrick Chandler that was setting off small explosions of awareness within her entire body. Her legs felt wobbly and her heart ached for something that had once been within her grasp and now seemed light-years away. She needed some air; she had to get out of here before she made a complete fool of herself.

"What if I told you that I wouldn't press charges against your brother?" His unexpected words halted her departure.

Had she heard him correctly? She turned and her puzzled gaze encountered his.

"What did you say?"

"I think you heard me."

"Don't toy with me."

An arrogant half smile turned up the corners of his mouth at her chastising tone.

"I never play, unless I choose the game and am assured of victory."

She believed him. He was a man used to getting his way—always, except once with her. She slowly walked back until she was standing in front of his desk again.

"So you're serious about letting Robert off the hook?"

"Yes."

Something in his tone worried her, yet she stood her ground. She had the feeling she would regret her next question, but she had to ask it.

"What do you want in return?"

He stood and slowly walked until he was standing in front of her, so close that their bodies were almost touching. She resisted a strong impulse to turn and run or take the few steps necessary to bring them breast to breast. She faced him unwaveringly as she waited apprehensively for his response.

His eyes roamed over her from head to toe. His blatant

inspection made her feel as if she were a piece of prime meat he was preparing to devour with that wicked mouth of his. Her heart began to beat erratically, not from fear, but from another emotion just as strong.

"Something only you can give me."

"Which is what?" She tilted her head up his tall frame, staring at him uneasily.

He continued to subject her to his slow scrutiny, his eyes lingering long on her moist, slightly parted lips, before lifting to meet her eyes once again. His thorough examination was more disquieting than anything she could have imagined he would say. However, his next words proved her wrong.

"I want you," he answered truthfully.

Chapter 2

He was unblinking and serious as he continued staring into her huge, horrified eyes. After a few seconds of silence, he laughed out loud at her apparent shock. He knew his declaration was the last thing she had expected to hear—it was honestly the last thing he had expected to utter.

She didn't make a move as his brief laughter reverberated in the quiet office before silence returned. He said nothing further and she was unable to respond. Instead, she stared at him unblinkingly, a hand slowly going to her suddenly constricted throat while her heart thudded loudly.

When she finally found her voice it was hushed and strained. "You can't be serious!"

"Can't I?"

She searched his face for signs that he was being facetious, yet found none. Still, he had to be joking. Her other hand moved to her throbbing temple and she tried to laugh dismissively—she couldn't have heard him correctly.

"I must have misunderstood you."

"Did you?" His piercing eyes studied her face carefully.

"Did you say that you want...me?" She forced herself to repeat his ridiculous statement.

"You understand me correctly."

"What do you mean by *want?*" As she articulated the question, she was petrified of his response.

"Want. A transitive verb meaning to desire, to have need for, to crave."

Every word he used to describe his meaning brought vivid pictures to her mind. She swallowed hard to dispel the lump that had rapidly risen in her throat, but to no avail. She stared at the man in front of her, amusement still twinkling in his eyes. Yet, underneath the levity lurked something else—a seriousness that terrified her.

"Are you saying you expect me to...you expect us to... that you want..."

She couldn't force herself to finish that sentence.

"I want you to marry me."

"Marry you?" She sank into the chair she had vacated earlier.

"What did you think I meant?" He studied her distraught face carefully. "Alesha, you didn't think I wanted us to live together in sin, did you?"

"Why do you want to marry me?" She needed a cold compress for her head.

"Because I need a wife." He reclined against his desk.

"You *need* a wife?" She paused before continuing. "Why?"

"According to my campaign manager, it would be good for me to be seen as a family man, and having a wife would equip me with a full-time hostess and date."

He took no pleasure in reiterating Cam's earlier words. Although seeing the woman who had single-handedly ruined his life two years ago in acute distress was very gratifying, indeed.

"How romantic."

Her dry tones made his eyebrow rise slightly—he had no clue how she managed to be sarcastic at a time like this.

"You once made it clear that you didn't want romance from me. Has that changed?"

"Do you always do what others tell you?" She deliberately sidestepped his previous question.

"Never." He firmly shook his head.

"Then why start now?"

She couldn't marry him—or anyone else—under these circumstances. The very idea was absurd!

"I've already answered that question." His face was unreadable.

"Have you?"

Of course, he didn't tell her that until she had walked through his office door, he had no intention of agreeing to Cam's suggestion. Even having put the proposal on the table, he couldn't believe he had done so. Yet, there had always been something about her—something that sparked a chord inside him. He was dismayed to learn his reaction to her hadn't dissipated with the time they had spent apart—time she had forced them to spend apart, he angrily went over in his mind. Despite his better judgment, he still wanted her, and this time he was determined to have her—all of her.

"You don't even like me."

She waited for him to respond but he remained silent. Slowly, he smiled without humor and neither denied nor confirmed her observation. Lord, she wished she had never come here today! She had thought, prayed, that time would have healed old wounds. However, it was painfully apparent it had not. He obviously wanted nothing to do with her, but if that was true, why was he suggesting that they get married?

"'Like' is irrelevant, Alesha."

"How can you say that? How can you suggest that we get married?"

"I told you why already."

He sighed, his tone implying he had no desire to explain his reasons to her again or to justify them to himself.

She lowered her aching head into her hands and willed herself to wake up from this nightmare. However, when she raised her head again, the man in front of her had not vanished, as she had hoped. Rather, his presence was undeniable as he watched her closely.

"You're serious."

"I am." He nodded affirmatively.

"Is this about revenge?" She articulated the only possibility that made any sense to her.

"It's about fate, Alesha."

"Fate?"

Her disdainful, soft echoing of his single prophetic word caused a slight clinching of his jaw—or did she imagine that?

"Yes."

There was uncomfortable silence as each tried to guess what the other was thinking. Each one of them would have been surprised to realize their feelings were more in sync than not. Since parting, they had been destined to come to this point and now they were here. Where their lives ended up from here was a mystery to them both.

"If I agree to your proposal, what do you expect?"

She couldn't believe she was actually contemplating his unorthodox proposition. However, she didn't have a viable alternative—not if she wanted to save her brother.

"Model behavior, public affection. There'll be a great deal

of publicity and we will have to appear happily married and very much in love."

Intense dread spread throughout her entire soul as he rattled off his requirements for a wife as if he were reading from a shopping list. He seemed so hard—had she done that to him? Somehow she knew she had and that hurt more than anything.

"And privately?" She stared into those cool gray eyes of his.

"You'll have to be more specific."

His mocking smile showed that he knew exactly what she referred to. He was getting immense pleasure in needling her.

Taking a deep breath and releasing it on a sigh she elaborated, "This will be a marriage in name only?"

"No, it will not."

She stood up at that, her chest heaving rapidly. "You can't expect me to…for us to…" Her voice trailed off, unable to finish that sentence.

"I can, and I do." His eyes swept appreciatively over her slender, shapely body.

"This is ridiculous, and I'm a fool for even considering your absurd proposition!" She turned and walked rapidly toward the door.

She had a right to be angry at his suggestion. He would have been disappointed if she weren't. He could have picked up the phone and had ten women in his office within a matter of minutes, willing to do whatever he wanted. But he didn't want any other woman. He wanted Alesha. Damn her, he always had. He didn't want to desire her, but he couldn't help it any more than he could help breathing. She intrigued him and he wanted the chance she had denied them both two years ago—to get to know each other better, intellectually and intimately. And, God help him, he didn't care that he was literally blackmailing her to get that opportunity.

He knew he was treading on dangerous ground—he also knew there was absolutely nothing he could do to stop himself. He craved Alesha, and this time he was going to do whatever it took to get her and to make her admit that she wanted him, as well. He wouldn't allow himself to dwell on why her desiring him was of the utmost importance to him.

"You're a smart woman, Alesha." His words halted her progress toward the door. "I think you know this is the only way to save your brother from a sure conviction and a lengthy prison term."

She slowly retraced her steps to stand several feet away from him and tried one last time to reason with him. "Mr. Chandler..."

"Derrick."

"Mr. Chandler." At her refusal to use his first name, she received another one of his mocking smiles, which she had quickly grown to hate. "We're virtually strangers. How can you expect me to marry you and become your wife in every sense of the word?"

"First of all, we are hardly strangers, Alesha. Secondly, when you grow a little older and a little wiser, you'll realize a lot of people do things that they don't want to do every day because their survival or the survival of those closest to them requires it."

"Is that supposed to make your ridiculous offer easier to accept?"

"You might surprise yourself and actually enjoy being married to me." He silently promised himself that would be the case.

She glared at him. "Never!"

"Never say never, Alesha."

He pushed away from the desk and walked over to stand

inches from her. Reaching out his hand, he trailed a finger lightly down her soft cheek, and he nearly groaned at the contact he had longed for since she had first entered his office.

She shuddered at his touch. He merely smiled before his finger moved to trace the outline of her lower lip, causing her flesh to tingle uncontrollably—and not from revulsion. His intense gaze mesmerized her and she was unable to step away, even when he removed his finger from her face. Ravenous eyes slowly, carefully studied every inch of her from the top of her head to the tip of her toes.

It was difficult to take in enough air to properly expand her lungs. Where his fingers had lightly touched, she burned and yearned for something forbidden. The spicy scent of his aftershave wafted up to her nostrils, causing her mouth to water. Despite her qualms, she wanted to be pressed close to his hard body and feel his strong arms around her.

She remembered how those lips had felt against hers and longed to see if her memories were accurate. She swayed toward him slightly, and he smiled even more, yet he made no further attempt to touch her, much to her dismay.

His inaction and her bizarre reaction to him cautioned her to get as far away from him as possible, but her limbs refused to obey the silent command. What was the matter with her? Was he hypnotizing her? Why didn't she turn and run away?

As his eyes admired her beauty, he knew exactly how she felt—he felt the same way, too. It didn't make any sense. This strong attraction between them was the last thing he needed, yet here it was, and he was absolutely helpless to do anything about it, except try to assuage it in hopes of finally purging it forever.

He continued his perusal, eyes moving to the soft curls of her hair, which was pulled away from her face by a clasp. He longed to free the soft tresses he knew would be smooth and silky. Her face showed the barest traces of makeup, yet her type of beauty didn't require any artificial enhancements. Her brown eyes were distraught, her smooth brown skin begged to be touched, her lightly tinted full lips were made for kissing— an invitation he had accepted often in the past and almost consented to now. The bulky sweater she wore hid her attributes from his piercing gaze, yet he knew from experience that beneath it was a curvaceous, beautiful body that he was certain would give him the most intense pleasure.

She could barely breathe. His eyes thoroughly destroyed her equilibrium as they sensuously appraised her. She didn't allow herself to speculate on his thoughts—knowing instinctively that they would disturb her more than his blatant perusal did. She felt hot, uncomfortable and something else she refused to put a name to.

"You're a beautiful woman, Alesha, but then you've always known that, haven't you?" His voice hardened perceptibly as his hand moved up to cup the side of her face, his lips mere inches from hers.

"How dare you!"

His condescending tone propelled her into action. She pushed his hand away from her face and moved several steps back, placing much-needed distance between them. She silently willed her wayward pulse to return to normal— impossible until she was no longer in his presence.

"You'll find that I dare quite a lot."

Silently, he promised himself he would taste those lips again soon enough. For, try as she might to find another way, his was the only course of action she could take to save her brother. He knew that and so did she. He was certain she would agree to his terms.

"What makes you so sure I will be around you long enough to realize anything about you?"

"Because your brother's life is in your hands. I think you'll do anything to save him—even marry me."

She was tempted to tell him to go to hell and take his demented proposal with him. Unfortunately, she knew it wasn't a question of whether she could live with his unreasonable proposal, but rather whether she could live with herself if she didn't even try. This was the only way to save the two people she loved most in this world.

He walked back behind his desk and sat down in his chair. He knew she loved her brother and would do anything to get him out of this horrible situation—her presence here was evidence of that. However, maybe this was too high a price for her to pay. But could she live with herself if she didn't try to help him? Could she live with herself if she did?

"If I agree to marry you, why can't it be a marriage in name only?" To her horror, Alesha blurted out a question that made it obvious she was considering his offer.

All she had to do was take one look at him to answer her own question. Derrick Chandler was a handsome, virile man. He wouldn't go without a woman for days, let alone months—he would never have to. Besides, their past relationship wouldn't allow him to marry her only for show. He wanted what she had denied him—of that, she was certain.

"Alesha, I expect our marriage to be real, because that's the way it has to be."

"Why?" She grudgingly admitted, "You're a handsome man. You can have any woman you want. Why me?"

"Thank you for the compliment." He smiled. "I'm running for public office. I can't be married to you and then be seen around town with other women." He felt compelled to add, "And I have no intention of living the life of a monk."

"But why me?"

"I think you already know the answer to that question."

He reclined in his chair, studying her distraught countenance.

"But…"

"I've got a lot of work to do."

His statement was true. However, more to the point, he needed to get her out of his sight so that his pulse could return to normal. This reunion was more upsetting than he had anticipated. Why, after the hell she had put him through, did she make him feel like a damn schoolboy asking a girl out for a first date?

"I'll give you twenty-four hours to decide. If I haven't heard from you by this time tomorrow, I'll take that as a no and contact the police."

He was proud his voice remained steady, when he felt anything but. He lowered his head and began to study the papers on his desk once again, totally ignoring her.

She opened her mouth to try to convince him to give up this ridiculous idea, but closed it again, realizing the futility of that gambit. He had set his terms and the next move was up to her. Without another word, she turned and left, slamming the door forcefully behind her.

He leaned back in his chair and let out his breath on a loud sigh. Tense fingers loosened his tie a bit. She hadn't left a moment too soon. Why had seeing her again affected him so profoundly? It was because he hadn't been with a woman in a while—that was it. That had to be it.

He shook his head in satisfaction and returned his eyes to the manila folder on his desk. After a few seconds, he gave up trying to concentrate on anything other than anxiously awaiting Alesha's return tomorrow, even though he already knew what her answer would be.

Alesha entered her mother's home and forced herself to appear happy and carefree, even though her heart was heavy, laden with the ultimatum Derrick Chandler had just issued to her a few hours earlier. Despite the dark cloud of gloom that hung over her, she could not risk letting her mother know she was upset—her mom had already had one heart attack a year and a half ago. Alesha would make sure she didn't find out about the events currently transpiring in her children's lives.

"Mom?" She searched for her mother as she walked through the house, throwing her coat onto a chair in the hallway.

"I'm in here, darling."

Following her mother's voice, Alesha made her way toward the bedroom. Once there, she was extremely glad to see that, for once, her mother was taking her doctor's advice, reclining in bed, though she was fully dressed.

Alesha walked over and kissed her mother's cheek warmly before perching lightly on the side of the bed. "How are you feeling?"

"I'm fine, darling." Barbara Robinson smiled as her daughter eyed her carefully.

Alesha marveled at what a beautiful lady her mother was. At age fifty-six, her black hair was sprinkled with gray and was cut short, attractively framing her oval face. Alesha smiled lovingly at her and silently vowed she would do everything in her power to make sure her mother stayed healthy and happy.

"What have you been up to today, dear?"

"Just the usual." She smiled. "Have you been following doctors' orders?"

"Yes, dear. I've been behaving." Barbara rolled her brown eyes heavenward. "Honestly, I don't know how much more rest and relaxation I can stand."

"Mother…"

"I know. I know." Barbara sighed heavily and then smiled slightly.

"You just continue to be a good girl, and Bobby and I will be around to make sure that you do." Alesha grasped her hand and surreptitiously took her pulse.

Before her mother could respond, the front door opened and closed and Robert's voice called out, "Mom? Alesha?"

"We're in here, Bobby." Alesha walked over to the bedroom door.

Seconds later her brother found them. He was about two inches taller than Alesha, though they both possessed the same café-au-lait coloring. Entering the bedroom, he bent down and placed an affectionate kiss on his mother's forehead, brought out a beautiful bouquet of colorful flowers from behind his back and handed them to her. Alesha noted and engraved in her memory the happy look on her mother's face. She would do anything to keep her that way forever.

"For the most beautiful lady in the world." He smiled as he straightened to stand beside the bed.

"They're lovely. Thank you." Barbara brought the bouquet to her nose and sniffed appreciatively.

"Let me get you a vase for them." Alesha took the flowers from her mother's hands and glanced pointedly at Robert, silently communicating that he should follow her.

"Is there anything sinful to eat in the kitchen?" Robert's brown eyes twinkled mischievously.

"Well, you know I'm not allowed," Barbara complained, "but, there is some chocolate cake."

"Perfect!" Robert smacked his lips in anticipation.

"Mother, what are you doing with a cholesterol-filled chocolate cake?" Alesha quickly returned from the doorway to glance at her mother disapprovingly.

"Relax, darling. I didn't eat any. Antonia came by today and left it. I couldn't turn her down, now, could I?"

"I suppose not." Alesha sighed before adding, "I'll be sure to take it with me when I leave—just to remove the temptation."

"Sorry, Mom, but you know how she is." Robert smiled sympathetically.

"I do, indeed."

"Don't you two start ganging up on me." She wagged her finger at them good-naturedly. "Come on and get your cake." Alesha pushed her brother ahead of her out of the room.

Robert's eyes focused on the cake sitting on the counter. "Mmm, this looks great!"

When the door was safely shut behind them, Alesha spoke slowly and calmly, "I went to see Derrick Chandler today."

"What?" He whirled to face her.

"Shh! I don't want Mom to hear you." Her voice was barely above a whisper, but firm.

"Why did you go see him? I thought you were going to stay out of this." He'd lowered his voice, yet his tone remained angry.

"You decided that, not me." She filled a vase with water. "I had to see if I could make him listen to reason."

"Did you?" He knew the answer before she replied.

Turning her back on him to cut a slice of cake, she replied cryptically, "In a way."

Robert walked around to stand in front of her, placing a finger under her chin and lifting her eyes level with his own. "What exactly does that mean?"

"He agreed not to press charges against you." She hoped he would leave it at that for now.

"If…" He knew there had to be an *if*.

She gave him his cake, took a deep breath and released it slowly before replying, "If I agree to marry him."

Robert nearly dropped the plate onto the countertop. He stared at his sister, horrified.

When he spoke, his voice was barely controlled. "Please, tell me you're joking."

She walked away from him to stare out the kitchen window. "I wish I was, but you know I wouldn't joke about this."

"Damn him!"

Alesha quickly walked to his side and placed a restraining hand on his arm. "Be quiet! Remember, Mom is just down the hall. We can't let her know what's going on."

When he spoke next, his tone was lower, but just as enraged. "I hope you told him what he could do with his idiotic proposal!"

She remained silent, lowering her gaze from his. Robert's heart skipped a beat at her demeanor.

"Alesha, you didn't agree to this insanity, did you?" He watched her closely.

She raised her eyes and responded truthfully, "He's given me until tomorrow to decide."

"There's nothing to decide. There's no way I'm going to allow you to sell yourself to him to save me! I knew what I was doing when I took that money. I'll suffer the consequences for it."

"Bobby, even though you were wrong to embezzle from him, I won't let you go to jail if there's anything I can do to stop it."

"I won't let you do this." He was equally unyielding.

"You can't stop me." She shook her head. "If Mother finds out what you did and you're sent to prison, the shock would kill her—you know that."

"But, Alesha…"

"No buts." She placed silencing fingers on his lips. "I can't risk losing either of you. If that means I have to marry Derrick Chandler, then I'll marry him." She wished she felt as calm as she sounded.

"You're a wonderful sister, but I will not allow you to marry someone you don't love to save me."

He turned and left the kitchen. She ran after him, but reached the front door only in time to see his car pulling away.

She closed the door and sighed. Her decision was already made—it had been the very second Derrick had made her the offer. She would do whatever it took to save her loved ones, even if it meant sacrificing herself in the process.

Cam's mouth was wide open in shock. "What did you say?"

Derrick laughed heartily before reiterating, "I'm getting married."

"To whom? When? How?" Cam shook his head vigorously as he fought to comprehend his friend's unexpected announcement.

"To Alesha Robinson and very soon." He chuckled at Cam's understandable confusion.

"Who?" He frowned as he racked his brain to put a face to the name he instinctively knew he should recognize.

"Robert Robinson's sister." Derrick played with the slender stem of his wineglass.

"Robert Robinson?" Then leaning closer to Derrick and lowering his voice so as not to be overheard, he asked, "The dude who embezzled from your campaign?"

"The one and only." Derrick nodded before bringing the glass of wine to his lips.

"Have you lost your mind?"

Cam's question was relayed so earnestly that Derrick couldn't refrain from laughing out loud again. He had laughed more today than he had in a very long time.

"You're the one who said I needed a wife." His gray eyes twinkled with merriment.

"I know, but…"

"Cam, this is perfect." His countenance was that of a kid set loose and given free rein in a candy shop. "It's a business arrangement, no emotional entanglements—just a plain, simple agreement that I will end once it's served its purpose."

It was also an opportunity he had waited two years for, a chance to exorcise the demons Alesha's abrupt departure had left in her wake. He was certain once he had some answers, and maybe even a measure of retribution, he would be able to permanently purge the tenacious memories of their past association from his mind and heart once and for all.

"Which is what?"

"To help me get elected, of course." Derrick sighed loudly. Boy, was Cam being dense tonight!

Cam's eyes took on a seriousness that was relayed by his next words. "Sometimes when we think we have something figured out, it takes on a life of its own and goes in directions we never expected."

"What am I going to do with you?" Derrick raised his eyes heavenward in exasperation at his friend's prophetic statement. "If I don't do what you suggest, I never hear the end of it, and if I take your advice, I get prophecies of doom and gloom."

"When I suggested marriage, I wasn't referring to the farce you're contemplating." Cam took a much-needed gulp of his wine.

"Never again." Derrick adamantly shook his head.

"Derrick, you're my best friend. I'd like to see you happy." He lowered his glass to the table.

"I appreciate that, buddy, and I am happy. I'm also going to marry Alesha—on my terms."

"She's agreed to this?"

"Not yet, but she will tomorrow." His voice was confident as he fingered the slender stem of his wineglass.

"How can you be so sure?" He couldn't shake the nagging feeling that there was more to his friend's inane proposal than met the eye.

"She doesn't have a choice. It's the only way to save her brother."

"She might surprise you. Maybe she'll decide the price is too high to pay." Cam played devil's advocate.

"She won't." His short response was delivered confidently.

"Why won't she?"

"As I said before, she doesn't have a choice." Derrick hadn't noticed his tone turn somewhat cold.

"I get the feeling you know this lady—very well. Have you met her before?"

"Two years ago." Derrick silently cursed himself for slipping up in front of Cam, of all people.

"Wait a minute." His eyes reflected understanding. "Is this the same Alesha you dated briefly?"

"She is." He didn't see any reason in denying it.

"The one you abruptly stopped seeing, which sent you into one of the longest and foulest depressed moods of your life?"

"You're exaggerating." Derrick took a suddenly muchneeded swig of his drink. Cam wasn't exaggerating. If anything, he was being kind.

"No, I'm not." Intense eyes bore into his. "You wouldn't talk about her—not even to me."

"There was nothing to say."

"Really? I didn't believe you then and I don't now."

"Cam, we dated once or twice, it didn't work out and we ended it." He silently cursed the nerve in his jaw that was pulsing erratically.

"We both know there's more to it than that." He refused to be silenced. "I was there, remember? I know what happened to you shortly after the breakup." At Derrick's continued silence, Cam asked, "Are you out for revenge?"

"Don't be ridiculous." Cam's astute observations and Derrick's own contradictory feelings as far as Alesha was concerned made him uneasy, although his words appeared confident.

"I think you should reconsider this."

"There's nothing to reconsider. I'm going to marry Alesha and that's that." Derrick's tone was firm and final.

"Derrick, are you sure…"

"Yes, absolutely."

"How do you plan to pull this off?" He knew when it was useless to try to reason with his friend, and this, unfortunately, was one of those times. "Alesha will be in the limelight *all* the time. I assume you realize the public must perceive your marriage as real."

"Of course." Derrick shook his head in agreement. "In public, we'll appear as a couple very much in love. You, Alesha, Robert and I are the only ones who will know about our arrangement."

"And what about privately?" Cam leaned forward, studying his friend closely. "What do you expect, and—more importantly—want from Alesha privately?"

"Mr. Chandler, it's time for you to take your place onstage." Both men turned in the direction of the man who interrupted them.

"Certainly."

Derrick smiled and stood, grateful to escape his friend's last probing question.

Chapter 3

The following morning Derrick was engrossed in work when the intercom buzzed. Without being told, he knew who was here to see him and his heartbeat quickened.

"Yes?"

"Sir, Ms. Robinson is here to see you."

"Please send her in."

Standing, he walked over to the door seconds before it opened, admitting Alesha. She opened her mouth to speak and then closed it again. He remained silent. This was her show.

She took a deep breath, released it and, before she lost her nerve, said, "I'll marry you."

"I see."

"You don't seem very surprised." She raised an arched eyebrow.

He ushered her over to a chair in front of his desk and then perched on the edge. "I'm not. You didn't have much of a choice."

"No, I didn't."

She didn't try to hide the resentment in her voice before angrily lowering her gaze from his. She was uncomfortable with him so close and wished he would move away. Yet, even as the thought entered her mind, she realized she would have to get used to being in much closer proximity than this to him—after all, they would soon be husband and wife. At that thought, she shuddered visibly.

"Are you cold?" His hand rose toward her.

"No."

Sensing her discomfort, he dropped his hand to his side, stood up, walked behind his desk and sat down. He smiled slightly as she breathed a silent sigh of relief.

"Do you have any questions?" He leaned back in his chair and studied her somber expression.

"Such as?"

"In case you've forgotten in the time we've been apart, my age, religion, likes, dislikes, etc."

"Tell me whatever you want."

He smiled slightly at her tone, which infuriated her. Why did he always act as if she amused him? He was so frustrating!

"To refresh your memory, I'm thirty-six, born and raised in Washington. I was an only child. My parents are deceased. My favorite food is Italian." He rambled off facts she was mortified to realize she still remembered.

"I'll make a mental note of all that."

"You do that." He leaned forward. "Let's discuss specifics, shall we?"

What he really wanted to do was touch her—to experience the softness of her skin for a much longer duration than yesterday's brief contact. He wanted to release her bountiful mane from its clasp, bury his face in the feathery soft tresses and see firsthand if they were as silky and soft as he remembered. He wanted to devour those pouting, luscious lips…

"All right, but I have one condition."

He raised an eyebrow. "You're in no position to make any demands."

His arrogance was born out of desperation rather than disdain. He didn't want to be cold with her, but it was either that or make a complete fool of himself by acting on his longings.

The hair on her neck stood on end at his insufferable tone. However, her voice was measured when she responded. "I realize that, but I really must insist on this one."

"What is it?"

"My mother must believe our marriage is real. I don't want to upset her."

Did she imagine the softening of his features at her sincere confession? That was ridiculous. He hated her and marriage to him would be his ultimate revenge.

Much to her surprise, he agreed. "Fair enough. Everyone has to believe our marriage is real—that includes your mother." At her continued silence, he said, "Anything else?"

"Yes." She paused, trying to find the best way to phrase her next request.

"Well…" He drummed his fingers on the desktop, not out of frustration or impatience, but to keep them from trying to touch her.

"I'd like us to be engaged for a few months so that my mother will buy our relationship."

His fingers immediately stilled. "Impossible."

"Why not?"

"I have a little over a year until the election. We must be married as soon as possible." He paused, considering a compromise. "I can give you a month at the most."

What he didn't tell her was that he doubted he could wait longer than that to quench his burning desire for her—he prayed he wouldn't go mad trying. Damn her and him! Why, after all that had transpired between them in the past, did she still have the power to unnerve him the way no other woman ever had?

"This will never work, you know." She shook her head.

"It will work." He smiled confidently. "Wait and see."

"If you say so." Her tone belied her skepticism.

"Do I need to remind you what I expect from this marriage?" His gray eyes bore into hers.

Nervously wringing her hands in her lap, she warily met his gaze. "No."

"You're positive?" He stood and walked slowly toward her until he reached her side.

"I'm positive." She also stood to be on a more level plane with him.

"Don't say you didn't know what to expect."

"Is there anything else?" She unflinchingly met his determined gaze.

"Just three things."

He motioned for her to resume her seat, which she did reluctantly. He perched on the desk in front of her. He wished she would stop looking so sad, as if she were being handed a death sentence.

"What are they?"

"First of all, I don't know whether you're on birth control or not, but if not, you will need to start immediately."

She felt her cheeks grow warm at his intimate demands. How could he expect her to discuss such things with him! His words made her fully aware of what their relationship would be, and all she could do was stare at him in embarrassment.

"Since this is only a business arrangement, neither of us needs or wants any unnecessary complications."

She found her voice and whispered resentfully, "Why is it always the woman's responsibility?"

"Well, I can't speak for other men, but as for me, I dislike the feel of a condom. I don't want anything to come between me and..."

"I'll take care of it."

She blushed hotly at his blatant admission, wanting to get off this subject as soon as possible. She reached up to touch her suddenly constricted throat.

He smiled at her as his eyes moved down her face to rest on her slightly quivering, espresso-colored lips, before traveling slowly back up to encounter her distraught eyes, and his smile deepened. However, there was something else present in her eyes—a deep longing, an expectation, a need. He saw it there, silently admitting that it echoed similar smoldering feelings within him.

She really was delicious. He had a feeling he was going to enjoy being married to her very much—while it lasted. He forced himself to mentally add the last observation and forcefully reminded himself that theirs would only be a brief alliance to purge her from his life once and for all. He didn't want or need anything more permanent.

"What's number two?" Her voice was breathless as she brought a hand up to her suddenly burning cheeks.

"It concerns your job." His tones took on an ominous ring.

"What about it?"

"You'll have to give it up."

Her eyes changed from wary to disbelieving to angry as she glared at him. He felt an absurd desire to pull her in his arms and tell her everything was going to be all right.

"Give up nursing? Why?"

"The main reason for this marriage is so that I will have a ready-made hostess. You'll have to be available at a moment's notice. That's hardly possible for someone in your profession."

"I love my work. I don't suppose that matters to you."

"I understand, and I know that you're very good at it." The sympathy in his voice was overshadowed by the sacrifice he was asking her to make.

"How do you know that?"

"Have you forgotten that I saw you in action when we first met at the accident scene?"

She remembered everything about their intense first meeting. It had been a multivehicle accident that both had stopped to help at. He had been strong, unshakable at the sight of blood and torn flesh and had been very receptive to taking orders from a woman.

"No, I haven't forgotten."

He had watched the play of emotions flit across her beautiful face. He wanted to ask if she remembered every detail of their breakup, too, but that was unnecessary. Finally having her in his presence again, he wanted to know why she had shut him out of her life. To this day, her rejection still rankled him, and that was one thing he was fighting tooth and nail to keep from her.

"What else do I have to give up?"

"Are you agreeing to my second condition, or do we end this right here?" His hooded eyes watched her carefully.

"Yes, what's your third condition?"

Her words should have thrilled him, yet instead they cut through him like a hot knife. He didn't know why he had the urge to apologize to her or why her understandable unhappiness made him so unhappy. He reminded himself that this was only a business arrangement, not an emotional entanglement. Either she agreed to his terms, or he would call the deal off and have her brother prosecuted. He wasn't forcing her to marry him. She had a choice—one he knew she wouldn't take—but a choice nonetheless.

"My third condition is this."

Unable to hold himself in check another second, he stood and slid one strong arm beneath her coat around her slender waist, pulling her closer as his other hand moved to the back of her head, pulling her lips toward his.

"What do you think you're doing?" She pressed her hands against his solid chest, trying unsuccessfully to break free from his unwelcomed embrace.

"You'll have to do better than this, or you won't convince anyone that you're madly in love with me." He lowered his head toward hers.

She continued to struggle in vain. However, when his lips were mere inches from hers, one hand released her silky tresses from their confining clasp, allowing the shoulder-length tendrils to slide over his fingers as he pulled her mouth toward his. As he had known it would, her hair felt like silk against his fingers. His appreciative eyes swept her distraught face thoroughly.

"I prefer your hair loose, remember?"

"Mr. Chandler, I don't care what you prefer."

"Oh, but you will care." His softly voiced promise caught in her throat as he once again instructed her to use his first name.

"No." She strained against his ironclad embrace.

"You'll say my name on moans of passion in just a few seconds."

"Never."

She knew her denial lacked believability because her voice was breathless, and a strange feeling began forming in her stomach at his nearness.

"We'll see."

Before she could respond, determined lips closed over hers in a strong kiss. His mouth was warm and inviting, not cold and repulsive as she had hoped it would be. She had known from past experience that his lips would feel like this—wonderful and vital. Days, months and years were swept away by his sensual mouth as it thoroughly refamiliarized itself with hers.

Her heart began to beat rapidly—not in fear, but in arousal. She moaned in protest to her thoughts and his actions, and her mouth parted slightly in shock and surrender.

That was all the encouragement he needed. He took full advantage of her surprise, sliding his tongue between her lips to slip into the honeyed recesses beyond. He continued to masterfully taste every centimeter, every tantalizing crevice of the bounty he had uncovered.

Her hands moved to his shoulders to push him away, yet stopped there, resting instead. Did she really want to escape? That simple yet complex question rolled around in her dazed mind. A hundred confusing sensations bombarded her entire being as Derrick continued his mind-shattering caresses. She hadn't expected to be blown away by a simple kiss after two years. However, there was nothing remotely simple about Derrick's kiss, or her disheartening responses to the masterful, sensual onslaught he was unleashing on her.

One of his hands slid languidly down her back to rest on her hip, pressing her closer against his hard length as his mouth continued to plunder hers. Her eyes were half closed, as sensation after sensation—each an awakening, each frightening and intensely pleasurable—began to overpower her self-proclaimed resentment of the man whose arms she was nearly melting into. The hands resting on his shoulders flexed and then tightened their grip as she resisted an almost irrepressible urge to entwine them around his neck and press herself even closer against his hard length.

Never in a million years would she have dreamed she would be in Derrick's arms again, enjoying his kisses and caresses. Yet, here she was, wanting, almost reveling, in this intimate contact with a man she should hate for blackmailing her into marriage. She hadn't bargained for this. She hadn't expected to still be attracted to him physically. How could this be? Even as the question arose in her mind, she admitted that he was the only man who had ever elicited such thorough, satisfying, mind-boggling passion from her and, to her dismay, he had lost none of his skills when it came to arousing her hidden desires.

His lips slowly drew apart from hers, despite a slight moan of protest from her, and he huskily commanded, "Say my name."

"No."

Her voice was soft and tortured. For the life of her she didn't know where the strength to articulate came from.

Her refusal made him pull her closer, until she felt every hard inch of his wonderful body pressed intimately, maddeningly against her own. Unapologetic hands slipped beneath her sweater to touch the satiny heated flesh of her back, and she thought she would die from something very close to rapture when he pulled her yet closer.

Playful lips nipped at hers before sliding down her jaw to burrow into her softly scented throat. She gasped as he raked his strong teeth across her skin, and then his tongue traced the outline of her collarbone before he raised his head to stare into her confused, dazed, passion-glazed eyes.

"Say my name." As he softly repeated his previous command, one of his hands moved to her hair, his fingers entangling there.

He was as surprised as she looked at the shock of pleasure

holding and kissing her elicited within him. It was as if the damnable time they had spent apart had never occurred. He pulled her mouth to within centimeters of his. His tongue skimmed her lips lightly before retreating again, refusing to give her what she wanted until she yielded to his demands.

"Say it."

His warm breath intermingled with hers as the hand at her back moved to rest between her shoulder blades before sliding back down her satiny flesh. He needed to hear his name on her lips, whispered with passion before he muffled the sound with his ravenous, hungry mouth.

She closed her eyes briefly before acquiescing. She spoke so softly he thought he had imagined it.

"Derrick."

"Again." He softly kissed her quivering lips—lips that were as addictive as anything he had ever known.

"Derrick," she reiterated on a sigh, and then on a moan, as he had foretold, as his lips and hands continued to lightly caress her. "Derrick."

The last thing she saw was his smile—not of triumph, but of understanding—before her eyes closed once her mouth was finally, ravenously recaptured. He kissed her again and again and she prayed he would stop soon before she begged him never to. His lips were like a magnet, attracting her against her will, holding her mesmerized, unable to break away.

The last thing she wanted was to escape from this intensely pleasurable embrace. Her mind screamed out for her to put as much distance between them as possible, yet her body craved closer contact with his—much closer. How could she remotely tolerate kisses from a man who was single-handedly ruining her career and stealing her freedom? What in the name of God was wrong with her? She couldn't begin to formulate an answer anymore than she could deny that she craved and enjoyed his kisses, almost to the point of self-destruction.

After endless, sweet minutes of torture, his firm, strong, warm lips dragged themselves from hers. She fought the urge to pull his mouth back to hers and gradually opened her confused, embarrassed eyes to find him staring at her with an unreadable expression. Her cheeks were warm, her lips were trembling, and she could just die from the embarrassment.

He smiled slightly, one of his fingers trailing over her quivering, moist lips as he huskily said, "I think our arrangement will be very profitable and pleasurable—for the both of us."

She pushed away from him at his words, partly in anger and partly just needing to escape from his overpowering presence and from her own desires. She needed to get out of there! This time he let her go, and this time she nearly ran out the door, not stopping to look back—certain she would find him following her.

Had she turned to stare at him, she would have seen echoing arousal, disbelief and dismay etched on his handsome features. Her retreating pace accelerated until she was safely out of his maddening reach—for the moment.

A few days later, she sat beside Derrick in one of the most upscale jewelry shops in Washington. Even though she had insisted she didn't want an expensive ring, he had been adamant that she would wear a ring to be marveled at, for appearances' sake.

She hadn't seen him since the devastating kisses in his office, yet the time apart had done nothing to ease her mind, nor squelch her anticipation of their next encounter. She didn't know what was the matter with her or who she was becoming. Even more unnerving, when she was with him, she wasn't sure she even cared.

"What about this one?" He held up a three-carat brilliant-cut diamond solitaire, set in a split band of platinum.

"It's beautiful but..." She carefully took the exquisite ring from his fingers.

"But what?" He eyed her closely.

"It's too expensive—all these rings are."

She placed the exquisite ring back onto the black velvet cover on the table next to the matching wedding band, which was inset with a carat of diamonds halfway around it, and the man's wedding band, which was a thick circle of brightly polished platinum with scrollwork over its surface.

"Nonsense." He smiled at her assertion. "Besides, when this is all over, you'll have something to sell that will bring you a nice piece of change."

She turned hurt and angry eyes on him. When she spoke, her voice trembled slightly, "Why did you say that to me? You know I'm not marrying you for your money."

The somewhat mocking smile on his face slowly faded as he realized he had hurt her. Part of him had meant to, but he derived no pleasure from the fact that he had succeeded. Instead he felt miserable about it. He wasn't a cruel person and there was no reason for him to act like one.

"Alesha, I'm sorry."

He cupped her sad face between his hands tenderly—more tenderly than he would have imagined himself capable of.

"Are you?"

Her whispered words implied she didn't believe him. She was, however, oddly moved by his unexpected and uncharacteristic apology.

"Yes, I am. Very." Soothing fingers lightly rubbed over her cheekbones.

"You wanted to hurt me." Her voice was barely audible.

"Maybe I did," he admitted softly, eyes never breaking contact with hers.

Despite knowing the reason, she would have asked him why. However, his lips lowered toward and captured hers. He kissed her softly, soothingly at first, but as if the barest contact with her mouth inflamed him, the kiss soon became passionate, and the hands on her face pulled her closer to his ravaging mouth.

Her own hands slid up to rest on his chest as she allowed herself to enjoy the wondrous sensations washing over her body as Derrick's expert lips and tongue continued to mate hotly with her own. He had to be the best kisser in the world, she dazedly thought as, against her will, his mouth slowly lifted from hers.

"Why are you always kissing me?" Her question was formed breathlessly against his lips, which still rested lightly against hers.

"Because I enjoy it and so do you." He earnestly traced the outline of her moist lower lip with his tongue, feeling her quiver. "You always did, remember?"

She did, but she wouldn't tell him that. She realized she didn't have to articulate it. He knew—just as he knew she wanted him to kiss her again and again.

"Derrick, I…"

"What?"

"Nothing." She shook her head, not knowing what to say—or to confess.

His eyes bore into hers as he continued, "Your mouth is made for kissing—soft, moist, sweet and tempting—like a ripe, juicy, luscious strawberry. It begs to be stroked, caressed…consumed." He ended his erotic assertion on a ravenous whisper before his lips slowly tasted hers again.

His sensuous, hypnotic words stole her breath. Her heart

began to beat erratically at his nearness and the vivid imagery he had created within her head. She couldn't have responded if she wanted to, and it was just as well because, as if to prove his point, his lips pulled at hers, tasting them, before closing over hers again. Of its own volition, her right hand moved up his chest to his shoulder, to rest at the nape of his neck as he continued his exploration of her quivering mouth.

His hands moved to her back as his lips continued to kiss hers. She sighed in pleasure and her mouth opened wider as he continued to taste the sweet nectar he found within.

She had forgotten where they were and so had he, until a loud cough interrupted what had become a heated, passionate embrace. To her disappointment, Derrick's lips reluctantly slid from hers as they both turned toward the sound.

"Excuse me." The salesman's embarrassed countenance greeted them as they simultaneously turned passion-glazed eyes in his direction.

Alesha quickly lowered her gaze from his, so embarrassed she would have moved away, yet Derrick's hands on her back wouldn't allow her to. As always, he seemed completely in control of the situation.

"Forgive us—we're very much in love." He smiled at the salesman, who nodded in understanding.

"Of course, it's such a joy to see." The man beamed at the two of them. "Have you decided on rings?"

"Yes, we'll take these." Derrick handed the man the most expensive set in the case, the one with the trillion-cut solitaire. Then, turning loving eyes to her, he said, "Right, darling?"

"Yes." She was surprised anything audible passed from her passion-constricted throat.

"Excellent choice, sir, madam." The man barely contained his enthusiasm. "Shall I wrap them for you?"

"The wedding rings, but she'll wear the engagement ring." Derrick lifted the solitaire off its black-velvet base and placed it onto Alesha's finger before lifting her hand to his lips and kissing it as his eyes bore deeply into hers. If she didn't know better, she would think he loved her dearly.

"The perfect ring for the perfect fiancée." He lowered her hand from his lips, but continued to stare into her bewildered eyes.

"Let's just see how that fits." The salesman took Alesha's hand from Derrick's to inspect the ring. "It looks like an excellent fit. How does it feel?"

"It—it's fine." Alesha's eyes were still mesmerized by Derrick's.

He reclaimed her hand, kissing it again before he abruptly stood. "Darling, I'll be right back." Then he followed the ecstatic salesman over to the register.

Once alone, she placed sweaty palms against her burning cheeks. Uneasily, she contemplated what had just transpired between her and the enigma who was her fiancé. Trembling fingers lightly touched her moist, thoroughly kissed lips.

God, what was happening to her? With confused, forlorn eyes, she stared furtively across the room at Derrick, and she felt a twinge of longing in the pit of her stomach. Unashamedly, she wished he were still seated beside her, kissing and caressing her. She glanced down at the twinkling diamond on her left hand and, for a moment, wished her engagement to Derrick was real instead of simply a business arrangement. She shook her head to dispel the vivid longing that suddenly invaded her soul for something forbidden and terribly exciting, which she feared only Derrick could give her.

She was treading on very dangerous ground and must take extreme care not to think of Derrick as anything other than a means to an end. Marrying him would ensure her brother's freedom and her mother's continued ignorance of what Robert had done—nothing else good would come from their union. She had to keep repeating the suddenly distasteful truth that he was using her, as she was him. There were no emotional entanglements or involvements as far as they were concerned and she didn't want any. If only she could believe her silent assertions.

Why couldn't she hate him? She wanted to—things would be so much simpler if she did. But she didn't. Perhaps it was the realization that her still-unexplained actions were the basis for his angry feelings toward her. She understood his anger toward her better than he did.

In her mind, two years ago she had done what was necessary when she had ended things between them. Yet the decision still plagued her, even after all this time. Therefore, how could it not affect Derrick the same way? Besides, Robert had stolen an enormous amount of money from him, and he had a legitimate right to want to extract retribution from both of them, didn't he?

She knew he didn't love her. At times, she was certain his feelings for her leaned more toward hatred. However, there was no denying that he wanted her physically, and she instinctively knew he wasn't happy about that. She knew Derrick wanted nothing to do with her on a permanent basis, just as she wanted nothing to do with him. However, she was forced to admit to herself that she came to life in his arms as she did at no other time.

After two years, he still had a power over her body and sometimes her mind, but she silently vowed that she would not let that power extend to her heart. She couldn't afford to lower her guard with him because their relationship— although once very real—was now only a sham, a farce, an emotionless business arrangement. She must never let herself forget that, because if she did, she would truly be in danger of losing her soul.

Chapter 4

"Is your sweet young man coming for dinner tonight?"

Barbara Robinson smiled at her daughter as they sat in the living room of her house. Robert glanced up from his magazine with a scowl, but made no comment.

"Yes, Mom." Alesha grimaced slightly at her mother's choice of words.

Of all the adjectives she would use to describe Derrick Chandler, *sweet* was certainly not one of them. She would have chosen words like *gorgeous, enigmatic* and *arousing*. She grudgingly admitted she would also add the word *kind* to the list of adjectives. For he had been unbelievably kind to her mother in the past two weeks since she had been told about their imminent marriage and, if she were completely honest, kind to her, as well. Her mother had taken to Derrick remarkably well—too well for Alesha's taste.

"I'm so happy for you, darling." Barbara's sincere words broke into her disturbing thoughts. "I like Derrick. He's a good man—strong, dependable—and very handsome." She tagged on the last comment with a laugh.

Yes, he was devilishly handsome and sexy, Alesha admitted. Yet, there was also a hardness to him that hadn't been present years earlier. She knew she was the one responsible for its creation—a source of guilt to her. Now she wondered if she could also possibly be the one to eradicate it.

"Thanks, Mom. I'm glad you like him." She forced a lightness in her voice she was far from feeling.

"How could I not like him after seeing how he dotes on you?" Barbara beamed proudly.

Alesha smiled at her, but remained silent. Yes, Derrick certainly played the role of the doting fiancé very well—too well for her taste. The memory of the many kisses they had shared over the past few weeks made her cheeks burn with embarrassment. Kisses? That was a tame word to describe their passionate, near-consummated encounters since they'd become engaged. She blushed hotly at the memories.

He was *always* touching and kissing her, always raising her to a fever pitch, yet refusing to go any further. Though she should have been happy about that, she was disturbed to admit she was not. Irrationally, she wanted to know the fulfilling promise his smoldering kisses hinted at and truthfully believed he was trying to drive her insane with unfulfilled longing. Much to her dismay, she couldn't wait to experience the conclusion of Derrick's devastating caresses and kisses. Instinctively, she knew it would surpass anything she had experienced in her life.

Dear Lord, she couldn't believe her thoughts! What was the matter with her? What had he done to her in so short a time and what would he do to her sense of self once they were married? Married! Her mind slowly repeated that word. Soon, very soon, she would be Mrs. Derrick Chandler. Her life would definitely change then, but for better or for worse?

Alesha stood as the doorbell chimed. "I'll get it."

She reached and opened the front door to Derrick.

"Hello, sweetheart." He smiled lovingly at her.

His easy use of the endearment caused her heart to somersault. He handed her one of the bouquets of flowers he held in his hands. With his free arm, he encircled her waist and placed a firm, passionate kiss on her soft, moist, waiting lips.

When he released her, she was breathing erratically. He whispered in her ear before escorting her into the living room with his arm still around her waist.

"Try to look happy."

She nearly told him she didn't have to try to look happy—she *was* happy to see him. Of course, that was only because he had presented a reason to escape from her disquieting thoughts, wasn't it?

"Derrick, how lovely to see you again."

"Thank you, Barbara. It's nice to see you, too." He released Alesha and bent to kiss her mother's cheek while handing her the other bouquet of flowers. "Hello, Robert."

"Derrick." Robert's voice was clipped. "Excuse me. I need to make a call." He shook Derrick's hand before walking out of the room.

Alesha sighed as she sat down in a chair near her mother. She could see why her mother liked Derrick—he was absolutely charming. He did know how to make a person feel special.

"Thank you. These are lovely." Barbara sniffed the flowers appreciatively.

"I'm glad you like them." Derrick straightened and sat on the arm of Alesha's chair, his arm draped along the back.

She tried to listen to the small talk going on around her, but Derrick's nearness was making that impossible. His arm moved from the back of the chair to rest on the nape of her

neck, absently massaging her tense flesh. Instead of soothing her, it had the opposite effect. He lightly caressed her
soft skin, driving her to distraction. She wouldn't give him
the satisfaction of knowing how much his actions unnerved
her. She didn't have to because he already knew—a fact that
was confirmed when she glanced up into his eyes.

"Darling, you're wearing your hair down, just the way I
like it."

"You like her hair long?" Her mother's query thankfully
saved her from responding.

"Oh, yes." Derrick's voice was a potent caress as he continued to lightly finger her silky tresses.

"I tried to get her to cut it, but she said it would be too
much bother."

They continued to discuss her as if she weren't present,
which suited her just fine. She didn't think she could formulate a coherent sentence if her life depended on it.

"I'm glad she didn't—I love it the way it is."

He bent down and brought a handful to his nostrils, inhaling its fresh scent. Then he let it trail through his fingers
back against her warm cheek, his fingers still absently playing with a handful of strands.

She stopped paying attention to the conversation alto-
gether at that point. Derrick's nearness and actions banished
any logical thoughts from her mind, replaced by desires only
for him. She wanted to reach up and bring his satisfying lips
down to hers, and once again feel the burning ecstasy of his
kiss.

"Isn't that right, darling?"

She glanced up at Derrick, who was smiling down at her
lovingly and if she didn't know better, she would honestly
believed he cared for her.

"I'm sorry, what?" She shook her head slightly as she
forced herself to refocus on the conversation around her.

"Baby, were you daydreaming about our wedding again?" His finger lightly trailed down her burning cheek.

She swallowed the lump in her throat and forced a smile to her lips. "I'm afraid I'm guilty as charged, darling."

"Your mother was asking where we were going to spend our honeymoon, and I told her we had decided to go to my house in the country for a week and take a *real* honeymoon later on." His eyes laughed at her once again.

"Yes, Mom, that's right." She didn't know how she managed to make her voice sound cheerful when she felt anything but. "Excuse me—I think I need to check on dinner."

"Sweetheart, you just checked." Her mother frowned.

"I—I know, Mom, but it was almost ready. I'll be right back." She stood and hurriedly left the room, but not before she caught a glimpse of Derrick's mocking eyes as he followed her. No doubt, he knew exactly what she had been thinking and feeling. Damn him and herself!

A short time later, they were all seated around the dining room table. Alesha, of course, sat next to Derrick. Her mother and Robert sat on the other side.

"Sweetheart, tell me the full story of how the two of you met."

Her mother's question took her completely by surprise. She had assumed her brief response weeks ago had satisfied her mother's curiosity. She nearly choked on the piece of food she had just placed in her mouth and hurriedly took a sip of water before turning to Derrick.

"Why don't you tell her, darling?"

"All right, baby." He lightly kissed her lips before turning to her mother. "Well, Barbara, Robert sent Alesha to my office to pick up a check for a television spot." He glanced at Robert who was silently fuming. "I was floored by her visit, but more so by her beauty." He paused, this time to stare appreciatively at Alesha, and she grew warm under his burning gaze.

After he knew he had made her thoroughly uncomfortable, he said, "I was surprised when she wanted to discuss my campaign strategy. I had taken one look at her and my brains flew right out of the window. I asked her out to lunch, and she accepted." He kissed her cheek before continuing, "One meal with her wasn't nearly enough. I knew I had to see more of her, and we began to date. It became apparent that we were both swept away. The rest, as they say, is history." Derrick finished his tale and, much to her mother's delight, picked up Alesha's left hand and brought it to his lips.

"That's so romantic!" Her mother eyed them both with pure happiness.

"Yes, Mom, so much so that I almost can't stand it."

Thankfully, her sarcasm was lost on her mother. Derrick merely smiled and gave her hand a little warning squeeze. God, how she amused him! His eyes strayed to her tantalizing mouth and he resisted an almost irrepressible urge to capture those tasty lips with his own and spend untold minutes feasting on every sweet curve. He couldn't wait until they were married, until she was legally his wife and intimately his woman.

"Why did you wait so long to tell me you were seeing Derrick?" Her mother directed the question toward her.

"Tell her what you told me, darling." Derrick's eyes danced with mischief.

"Well, Mom, it was because…because everything happened so fast and we wanted to be sure about how we felt before we said anything." Alesha rattled off what she hoped sounded like a plausible answer.

"I understand." Barbara sighed as she glanced approvingly at the loving couple before her.

I'm glad you do, Alesha silently thought. Would this dinner never be over with? All she wanted was to get away from Derrick's disturbing presence, her alarming reactions to him, Robert's understandably sulky mood and her mother's glowing countenance as she bought into every shameful lie and half truth they fed her.

"It's partly my fault, too, Barbara. I was just getting to know Alesha, and I wanted her all to myself. I hope you can forgive me." He placed a lingering kiss on the corner of Alesha's mouth.

"Of course I can, Derrick."

Robert couldn't take another second of this nauseating display and quickly stood. "I hope everyone will excuse me, but I have to leave."

"So soon?" His mother frowned.

"I'm sorry, Mom. I thought we'd be through with dinner by now, and I have other plans." If he stayed here another second, he would surely throw up.

Derrick took everyone by surprise as he stood up, too, and said, "Robert, I was going to ask you this later, but since you're leaving, I'll just do it now."

"What is it, Derrick?" Robert tried to hide his dislike of the man for his mother's sake.

"Alesha and I have thought a lot about this, and we want you to be the best man at our wedding."

"What?"

Derrick thoroughly surprised everyone present. Robert and Alesha stared at Derrick in absolute shock.

"Oh, Derrick, how wonderful," Barbara said with great enthusiasm. "Isn't it, Robert?" She prompted him to respond to Derrick's offer.

"Are you sure, Derrick? Don't you have someone else you'd rather have stand up for you?" Robert tried to gracefully decline.

"Of course I'm sure. After all, you were instrumental in us getting together." Derrick smiled as he took Alesha's hand, causing her to stand before pulling her close to his side. "If it wasn't for you, we never would have become engaged."

"What about Cam?" Robert searched for a way out.

"He'll understand why I want you." Derrick refused to relent. "What do you say?"

"Sure." Robert glanced helplessly at Alesha who shook her head in resignation. "I really have to go now." He bent down to kiss his mother's cheek, and then dashed out the door.

"Derrick, that was so nice of you." Barbara continued to sing his praises, much to Alesha's dismay.

"It was nothing, Barbara. As I said to Robert, he's the reason Alesha and I are getting married. I can't think of anyone who deserves to be my best man more than he does."

Alesha stared at him, trying as hard as she could to hide the anger consuming her. He brought out such a range of emotions in her—one moment he could make her feel intense longing and desire. In a millisecond he could elicit a feeling of understanding and deep friendship. Just as quickly as he did now, he could spark a flame of anger, burning so brightly that she thought it would consume her. Her eyes blazed fury into the smiling, mocking depths of his.

At this moment, she was convinced that his sole purpose on earth was to bring chaos and disorder into her family's lives. His smile intensified, as if reading her mind, and somehow she resisted an urge to pick up her fork and use it as a weapon against him.

After dinner, Derrick sat on the sofa as Alesha paced angrily back and forth in front of him. Obviously, she was angry and he knew why.

She spoke to him in hushed, incensed tones. "You really enjoyed yourself tonight, didn't you?"

"Very much." His eyes followed her tense body as she walked away from him.

"How could you ask Robert to be your best man? You deliberately placed him in an untenable position." Her voice was angry, yet deliberately low enough so as not to disturb her mother.

"He could have said no."

"How? Momma would have become suspicious if he had."

"I hardly think Robert is the injured party in any of this."

"You're right about that." She stepped away and took several deep breaths. "Derrick, please reconsider. You don't want to marry me."

He stood at her words and walked over to face her. "On the contrary, I do."

"Why?" She was both flabbergasted and pleased to hear sincerity in his voice.

"Because you amuse me." He intentionally left unspoken the fact that she also inflamed, excited and captivated him.

"How flattering!"

"What do you want me to say? That I'm madly in love with you?" She remained silent and he continued, "You know why I'm marrying you, Alesha—it's purely business."

Even as he spoke the carefully chosen, cold words, he knew he was lying to both of them.

"How can I forget?" she hissed angrily. "You remind me every time I see you."

"You sound upset." He placed a hand under her chin and forced her turbulent eyes to meet the piercing depth of his own.

"Don't be ridiculous." She snatched her chin away, disturbed by his nearness and his insightful statements.

Despite her vehement denial, she knew he was right—she hated hearing him refer to their marriage as nothing more than a business arrangement, even though she knew that was exactly what it was. She tried to walk around him, but he grabbed her upper arm, stopping her.

"Maybe this is what you want to hear." He paused for what seemed like an eternity. "I want you, Alesha, very much. I've wanted you for a very long time, and this time I'm going to have you—all of you."

Her breath caught in her throat at his blatant, unexpected admission and arrogant assertion. She tried unsuccessfully to quash the vivid erotic images that sprang to mind as a result of his confession.

He moved closer until he was standing mere inches from her, causing her breathing to increase. Her heart thundered loudly in her ears as she continued to meet his scorching gaze. His hands reached out and grabbed her shoulders, pulling her body closer to his own.

"There's no one around to impress." She silently cursed her voice for sounding expectant and aroused instead of angry.

"I know that." He shook his head in agreement. "I'm doing this simply for my own pleasure—and yours."

He made her wait for an eternity until his burning mouth finally covered hers. She promised herself she would not respond. However, she soon found that her traitorous body had its own agenda. His hands moved to her lower back, pressing her intimately against the rock hardness of his own body. His tongue barely touched her lips and they parted, allowing him unlimited access to the hidden, inviting caverns of her sweet mouth. His hot tongue scalded hers.

Despite herself, she heard a moan of pleasure escape from her mouth and her arms slowly moved up his chest until they were entwined around his neck. He smiled slightly before pulling her up until she was standing on her tiptoes as he sucked her lips against his and massaged her tongue urgently with his own. Never in her life had she been kissed so thoroughly or devastatingly. Each kiss was different, yet achingly similar. When it came to arousing and satisfying a woman, Derrick Chandler was no novice, but then she already knew that. Without even trying, he could ignite her desire for him.

The hands at her back moved to trail lightly up her sides, resting at her breasts before sliding between her shoulder blades, pressing her closer as he continued his devastating assault on her mouth. She felt a similar sensation to one she hadn't known of until he had first kissed her, as the way he was now, building in pit of her stomach. It was a type of hunger, not for food, but for something entirely forbidden.

Her fingers fastened behind his head, holding him close. Her lips opened wider beneath the insistent, maddening pressure of his. Their kisses deepened. God, she wanted... What? What did she want? Something she was afraid to name, something she knew only he could give her.

Reluctantly, his lips slid from hers, and he stared deeply into her half-opened eyes. He studied the play of emotions dancing in their brown depths, and knew she was disturbed by her strong attraction to him. He himself was a little surprised and even troubled that, after all that had transpired between them, she still had the power to make him lose control.

The reason he kept reminding her about why they were marrying was that he needed to be constantly cognizant of that. Still, regardless of how they had come into each other's lives again, he couldn't wait for her to become his in every sense of the word. And though she would never admit it, he knew she was also anticipating the day when they would be husband and wife, but, more important, lovers.

His lips claimed hers again in another scorching kiss. Her eyes closed against the blinding passion mirrored in his, and she sighed in rapture against his bruising lips as they continued to devour hers. His fingers entangled in her hair, pulling her mouth closer still as he continued to savor her enticing lips. One of his hands moved to pull the hemline of the burgundy blouse she wore from the waistband of the matching skirt, sliding beneath to caress the warm, satiny skin of her lower back. She gasped against his mouth at the intrusion, but instead of moving away, she wantonly pressed closer, suddenly wishing their clothes would disappear, leaving only their bare bodies. She didn't know what was happening to her common sense, and at this moment, she didn't really care.

He felt her total surrender. He knew he could take her now and she wouldn't resist. For that reason, he also knew he couldn't, regardless of how much he longed to do so. He had silently promised himself not to consummate their relationship until they were married. He had convinced himself it was because he wanted to give her time to get to know him again, but the truth was that he was afraid that once he made her his, he would risk losing himself. He wanted... What did he want from her? Revenge, retribution or something simpler yet much more complicated and disturbing?

"I can't wait until we're married."

His admission was whispered against her moist lips. His mouth was so close to hers, she could still feel its imprint. There was no mistaking his meaning, and that prompted her eyes to flutter open as she stared at him, embarrassed by her actions and the fact that she hadn't wanted him to stop kissing or caressing her. Even now, her skin tingled from the light trails his fingers had blazed across it.

Unexpectedly, she pushed out of his arms and hotly responded, "Well, we're not married yet!"

She was angrier with herself for responding as eagerly as she had than she was with him for initiating the kiss. Turning her back on him, she prepared to leave him standing there alone. However, his hands prevented her from moving. He pulled her back and turned her around until she faced him again.

"But soon."

He placed a quick, hard kiss on her moist lips before he left her standing there alone, staring after him longingly, with nothing but her disturbing thoughts to torment her already tortured soul.

Chapter 5

Alesha sat in the hospital lounge, dressed in pale pink scrubs, checking the surgery schedule for the day. She tried unsuccessfully to ignore the envious banter of the four friends and colleagues who shared the lounge with her.

"Alesha, you're so lucky!" one of her friends cooed as she passed around a copy of *Time* magazine with Derrick's handsome face on the cover. She had to admit the eight-by-ten glossy photo from which the cover image was taken didn't begin to do him justice.

"How did you ever land such a marvelous catch?" the woman continued.

Returning her eyes to the schedule on her lap, she responded, "Just fortunate, I guess."

"I'll say you were!"

She sighed at the response. The slight sarcasm in her voice had been lost on her friends, who continued to salivate over Derrick's picture.

"Angie, you're on with Dr. Ryan at 3:00 p.m. in O.R. 12." She tried to redirect everyone's attention from her private life and back to work.

"Fine." The slender brunette with the short-cut hair nodded before returning to the subject that was on everyone's minds. "Come on, Alesha. Out with the dirt."

She looked up at her best friend, her exasperation evident. "What dirt, Angie?"

"How is he in the romance department? I'll bet he knows exactly what to do and does it expertly."

Alesha blushed at the explicit question, especially as she remembered the many ardent kisses she and Derrick had exchanged. What would Angela say if she told her she had never slept with Derrick—or with any man? She wanted to confide in her best friend. She could use some guidance in the romance department.

"Angie, leave Alesha alone. Can't you see you're embarrassing her?" said Linda, another one of her friends.

"I'll bet she could tell us all stories that would have our hair standing on end!" Angela picked up the magazine to take a closer look at the gorgeous man on the cover. "You'd better hold on tight—he's one sexy guy!"

"Why, thank you."

All heads turned in the direction of the door, to find the object of their conversation and desire lounging against the door frame, dressed impeccably in a charcoal suit, crisp white shirt and red tie.

"Derrick, what are you doing here?"

Alesha automatically stood and walked over to him. Dear Lord, how long had he been standing there and how much had he heard?

"I couldn't wait until tonight to see you, darling."

To the delight of her friends, he placed his hands around her slender waist, pulled her close and lowered his head purposefully toward hers. As always, they shared a breathtaking kiss. She clung to the lapels of his suit as she once again experienced the passion in his embrace. She didn't know how long he kissed her—time was suspended—however, when he finally lifted his head, she was more embarrassed than ever. She was sure that the blatant desire on his face, and hers, must be obvious to everyone in the room.

"Ahem!" Someone coughed loudly, making both of their heads turn in the direction of the other occupants of the room.

"Mr. Chandler, it's a pleasure to meet you." Never one to be accused of being shy, Angela walked up to shake his hand.

"Derrick." He smiled at them all in turn as they introduced themselves. "Please forgive me for interrupting your break."

His hand resumed its possessive position on Alesha's waist. He kissed her on the cheek.

She leaned against his chest and looked at him adoringly before plastering a stupid grin on her face, something she had gotten very good at in the last month. She hoped no one would ask her anything, because she didn't think she could trust herself to speak.

"It's no intrusion at all."

Alesha glanced at all of her friends as they nearly swooned at Derrick's feet. He could ask any of them all to jump out the fifth-floor window and they would do so gladly.

"I hope to see all of you at the wedding." At their gleeful promises, he added like a true politician, "And I hope I can count on your votes."

"Thank you. We wouldn't miss it for the world. And you definitely have my vote," Angela said, and the others promised to support him at the ballot box, as well.

"We can hardly wait for the big day ourselves." Derrick pulled Alesha closer. "Right, darling?"

All she could do was nod because, as always, his nearness was affecting her ability to think clearly. She wished he would let her go so she could breathe again. As if sensing her unspoken desire, and doing just the opposite, he pulled her even closer.

Everyone else reluctantly returned to work. Alesha would have gone with them, but Derrick refused to release her. Once they were alone, she turned to stare at him angrily.

"Was that really necessary?" She suddenly found her elusive voice.

"What?" He feigned innocence.

"You know what—that nauseating scene you just played."

"Weren't there a few parts you enjoyed?" His voice was slightly husky as he traced the outline of her trembling lower lip with the fingers of his free hand.

Despite herself, she felt a shudder pass down her spine to the tips of her toes at his touch and was certain he felt it, too. She longed for his lips to recapture hers once again.

His eyes shifted from hers to her slightly parted lips and back to her eyes again, yet he made no move to kiss her. Why was he toying with her? More importantly, why was she quivering in anticipation, craving another of his devastating kisses?

"Do you know what I want right now?" His voice was a whisper—his lips were a hair away from hers.

"What?" She fought to keep herself from swaying toward him.

Without answering her, his lips brushed against hers before he released her waist. Taking her hand instead, he led her out of the lounge into the busy hallway.

"Where are we going?"

They got onto the elevator. She glanced out to find all her friends watching enviously.

"To lunch."

"I can't leave the hospital. I have surgery in an hour and a half." She tugged against his hand.

"You'll make it. We're going to the hospital cafeteria." His smile widened as the doors closed.

After a brief stop at her office, which Derrick insisted on seeing, they boarded the elevator again. When it stopped on the twelfth floor, Derrick grabbed her hand and pulled her out.

"Where are we going? The cafeteria's on the first floor."

"You'll see."

He smiled and led her toward the doctors' conference room. A sign reading "In Use" was posted, but he disregarded it and began to open the door.

"Derrick, what are you doing?" Her hand covered his to stop him. "We can't go in there!"

"Of course we can." He swung the door open and ushered her inside.

She was still trying to reason with him when suddenly all her friends and colleagues ran toward them, yelling, "Surprise!"

They all beamed at her shocked face as she looked around the room, seeing for the first time that it was decorated with streamers, balloons and signs wishing her well. She quickly returned her astonished gaze to Derrick.

"You knew about this?" she gasped.

"Knew about it?" Angela walked over and hugged her tightly before continuing. "He's been a doll! We invited him, and he assured us he would be here, whenever, wherever."

"I—I don't know what to say." She stared at him in disbelief before quickly turning and adding to everyone, "Thank you all so much."

She was bombarded with hugs, well wishes and gifts. Someone shoved a glass of punch into her hands. Derrick was by her side constantly as she spoke with everyone. However, someone ushered him away to talk politics, and she was alone in the midst of another group of friends. Despite their good intentions, their words began to make her feel uncomfortable. She felt like a hypocrite, allowing people she had worked with for years to believe she was blissfully happy about her impending marriage, when nothing was further from the truth.

"Alesha, what's wrong?" Angela grabbed her hand in concern as she noticed the pained expression on her friend's face.

"Nothing, nothing." She forced a tearful smile.

"This is your best friend you're talking to. Tell me." She squeezed her fingers comfortingly.

"Oh, Angie, it's just…" She paused.

Even though Angela was her best friend, she had never spoken to her or anyone about Derrick—not two years ago, and certainly not now. How could she explain her inner turmoil to her friend, or to anyone here? No one could begin to understand what she was going through except…Derrick.

She searched for him, longing to be with anyone with whom she didn't have to pretend to be happy about leaving a job she loved in only two days. Her eyes encountered his as he stood across the room speaking with the head of surgery. He smiled at her reassuringly, and she automatically returned his smile. As odd as it sounded, she suddenly was very glad he was here. Her feelings were so complicated as far as he was concerned. Even though a part of her vowed to dislike him—a promise she had, thus far, been unable to keep—more times than not she enjoyed his company. That was a scary admission.

"What is it?" Angela's persistent tugging on her hand forced Alesha to refocus her attention.

"I'm just going to miss everyone so much." She hoped that would appease her friend.

"It's not as if you're never going to see us again. Besides, you'll be so busy with your handsome new husband and your exciting life that you won't give us a second thought."

"You may be right." She forced herself to assume a teasing demeanor.

She turned to respond to a question from another friend and, seconds later, felt a strong arm around her waist. She knew the arm belonged to Derrick. Her friends tactfully excused themselves, and she turned to face her soon-to-be husband.

He lowered his head and kissed her softly on the lips. "You looked like you needed rescuing," he whispered, his sympathetic eyes staring into her pained ones.

"I'm fond of all of these people—this is really hard."

"I know." He pulled her slightly closer.

Her hands automatically rested on his broad chest as she gazed into the compassionate depths of his eyes. In that instant, she felt that everything was going to be all right. To everyone present, they looked totally in love with each other.

"Why did you agree to come to this party?" She felt and heard him sigh as he studied her face.

"It was a good opportunity to test how others react to us as a couple." He deliberately chose his words to see how she would respond.

"I should have known," she hissed softly.

"If I had refused after being invited, it would have looked suspicious."

His words enraged and saddened her. She should have known he had only been thinking about his career! Anger darkened her eyes and she tried to free herself from his suddenly unwanted embrace.

"We certainly wouldn't want that." She tried in vain to free herself. "Will you let go of me?"

"Alesha, stop struggling before someone notices." His voice was low, but firm, commanding obedience. Yet she refused to comply.

"Let go!" She brought her free hand up to his chest and pushed. He moved his hand from her waist to her back, effectively sandwiching the hand on his chest between their bodies.

"There is another reason I came." He placed his free hand underneath her defiant chin and lifted her angry eyes to meet his.

"I don't care to hear it." She tried unsuccessfully to free her chin from his grasp.

She couldn't stand to hear any more of his heartless comments. She needed kindness from him, not taunting.

"I'm going to tell you anyway." He brushed a brief hard kiss on her lips, his hand moving from her chin to cup her jaw.

"Please stop, Derrick."

"I know it's hard for you to give up your career, even if just for a little while." His fingers softly caressed her cheek. "I thought today, of all days, having at least one person here with whom you didn't have to pretend to be happy about that choice—even if it was me—would make this farewell somewhat more bearable for you."

She immediately stopped struggling to free herself, but remained silent, unable to believe her ears. She searched his face for signs of teasing or deceit, and instead found only sincerity. He had articulated her feelings perfectly. How could he be so in tune to her feelings? How could he be both the cause of her pain and the only means to alleviate it? He never ceased to amaze or confuse her.

"What?"

"Contrary to your belief, I really don't want to make this any more difficult than it has to be." Fingers absently brushed stray strands of hair away from her eyes before he ruefully added, "I don't suppose I could expect you to believe that."

She stared at him, speechless, for a few moments before finding her voice. "I do believe you."

"Well, that's progress, isn't it?" He softly kissed her and she automatically responded to the warm, comforting pressure.

"I guess it is." She couldn't remove her gaze from the genuine tenderness reflected in his eyes, directed toward her.

"Did I tell you how beautiful you look tonight?"

"No." Her eyes registered surprise at his question.

"Well, let me remedy that." He took her hand and brought it to his lips. "You look gorgeous."

"Thank you." Her voice was wispy soft. "You don't look too bad yourself."

"Thanks."

He treated her to one of his devastating smiles before turning his attention to the traffic he was expertly weaving in and out of. They drove on in silence for a while. She had easily slipped into the role of Derrick's fiancée.

He pulled his sports car up to the restaurant and turned to face her. "Now remember, I told Cam that we met again..."

Alesha's fingers on his lips halted his words. "Derrick, you've told me a hundred times. I won't forget."

"I'm being a pain, huh?" He captured her hand with his own, refusing to release it.

"A little bit." She was breathless. Suddenly the close confines of the car became suffocating.

"I'm sorry." His eyes darkened.

"Um, I guess we should go in." Instead of moving away, an invisible magnet drew her closer to him.

"I guess."

Though he agreed with her, neither of them made any move to leave. Inevitably, they kissed. Lightly, at first, but then the unexpected passion consumed them. Her hands rested on his chest and he cupped her face, tilting his head one way and then another, bringing her sweet mouth closer.

A cool blast of air forced them slightly apart. "I beg your pardon sir, madam," A red-faced doorman apologized.

As always, it was Derrick who regained his composure first, glancing over her shoulder. "It's no problem. We were just getting out." Then, returning his attention to her, he asked, "Ready?"

She ran her tongue over her slightly damp lips, tasting him and nodded slightly. She didn't trust herself to speak. He released her face and opened his door before walking around to help her out. He continued to hold her hand as they entered the restaurant, where they were to meet his best friend.

As their coats were checked, Alesha used her fingers to wipe off traces of her lipstick staining his lips. Their eyes met and held for several suspended seconds before they were shown to a table. At their approach, a tall man who closely resembled her fiancé in build and height stood. He was dressed like Derrick in a dark navy suit with a red tie. He smiled easily, and Alesha instantly liked him.

"Well, well, I don't believe it. You're on time." The man chuckled at Derrick and then turned to Alesha. "It must be due to your good influence."

"Very funny." Derrick smiled. "Cameron Stewart, Alesha Robinson."

"Alesha, it's a pleasure." Cam shook her hand warmly. "Derrick said you were beautiful, but not exquisite."

"Thank you. I'm glad to finally meet you, Cameron." She smiled as he brought her hand to his lips briefly before releasing it.

"Cam. No one calls me Cameron except my mother—and Derrick when he's mad at me." He winked at his friend.

"Which you take deep pleasure in making sure is often," Derrick said as they were seated in the booth.

"Untrue." Cam shook his head. "I'm the easiest person to get along with you will ever meet."

"Hah!" Derrick snorted good-naturedly.

That was the way their dinner progressed. It was quickly apparent that Derrick and Cam were the best of friends, and could talk to each other only as best friends could and get away with it. Alesha enjoyed herself very much. She saw a side of Derrick that was completely relaxed—one she hadn't seen in a long time and one she liked very much.

Cam was a gem. He had a natural talent for making people feel at ease. Alesha took to him like a bee to honey. She felt a bit uneasy about deceiving him, but as Derrick had continually drilled into her head, everyone—including their friends and family—had to believe they were very much in love.

"Alesha, may I have this dance?" Cam stood and extended his hand in her direction after giving a chivalrous bow.

"I'd love to." She kissed Derrick's cheek. "You don't mind, do you, darling?"

"No, but you will once you experience his two left feet."

"He's just jealous because I'm a much better dancer than he is."

He *was* jealous, but not of Cam's dancing skills. Rather,

that Cam would be holding Alesha in his arms—something he himself longed to do.

"In your dreams." Derrick's words trailed after them as they walked away.

"Well, what do you think?" Cam glanced expectantly at Alesha as he twirled her around the dance floor.

"Very nice." Alesha smiled.

"You be sure and tell Derrick that." He winked at her and she laughed.

"I will." She returned his smile.

"You know, Alesha, I was blown away when Derrick told me he was getting married—and to whom."

"Were you? Why?" She feigned innocence, reminding herself to keep her answers short—there was less chance of slipping up that way.

"It was so sudden." Cam's words were an understatement. "Also, given your past relationship, it was the last thing I expected to happen."

"Our decision to get married is anything but sudden." Cam's dubious stare forced her to elaborate. "It took us two long years to realize we were destined to be together."

"Is that how you feel? As if you and Derrick were destined to be together?" Cam watched her with the attention of a hawk, studying its prey.

"Yes." She smiled at him and prayed for a change in topic.

"Really?" He twirled her out of the way of an approaching couple.

"Yes." She faced his piercing stare that was very similar to Derrick's. "I realize you don't know me very well, Cam, but believe me, I'm marrying Derrick because I want to."

"What's changed between now and two years ago?" He had skillfully maneuvered them into a relatively secluded part of the dance floor so that their conversation wouldn't be overheard.

She almost laughed out loud at his question. She wanted to ask how much time he had for her to list the monumental changes that had occurred in her life over the past two years.

"A lot." She silently cursed herself because even to her ears her voice sounded strained.

"I'm not prying just to stick my nose into yours and Derrick's business, Alesha." His voice was a little defensive.

"I realize that." And it made her feel all the worse for lying to him. "You're Derrick's best friend, and I know you have his best interest at heart."

"I do."

"For reasons I don't want to get into, Derrick and I weren't ready for each other two years ago. Now we are and we know what we want." Her words held shades of the truth and thus were spoken confidently.

"And that would be each other?" She felt as if she was on the witness stand and the case would be made or broken by her next words.

"Yes. Nothing else will satisfy either of us. We've finally realized that, thank God." She prayed for the music to end, because she didn't know how much more of this grilling she could take.

"Well, I suppose it's the romantic beginning and ending to a relationship any woman would love to have." Cam suddenly smiled and she heaved a sigh of relief.

"Yes."

"So it would seem that this time true love triumphed in the end."

He studied her closely—too closely. She realized this was the moment she would either sell the lie or destroy it.

"It has. I finally realized that Derrick is everything I want in a man and in a husband."

Her expression was appropriately dreamy as her eyes

sought out Derrick's from across the room. She sighed happily before returning slightly watery eyes to meet Cam's.

"I'm happy for you both." Cam smiled.

"Thank you." She gave a silent prayer. Apparently, he was buying her nauseating performance.

"No, thank you for returning to Derrick's life."

His words made her feel like a first-class heel. He was a nice man and a loyal friend, and she truly hated deceiving him. Even reminding herself that it was necessary didn't help salve her heavy heart.

"I like you very much, Cam."

"I like you, too." He smiled. "I see why Derrick jumped at the chance to marry you."

No, you really don't.

"Thanks." She smiled.

The song ended a few moments later, and they made their way back to Derrick.

"What were you two talking about so earnestly?"

"I was trying to steal her away from you." Cam winked at Alesha.

"Never happen," Derrick said.

Derrick placed a possessive arm around her shoulders and pulled her close. Absently, his fingers played with the strands of her hair.

"Sure of himself, isn't he?"

Cam smiled. He wondered if Derrick realized that he was always touching Alesha, or how his expression softened when he looked at her. His friend was in for a big surprise if he thought his marriage to Alesha was going to be a cold, antiseptic business arrangement.

"Very. But he's right, I'm afraid." Alesha joined in their infectious banter, placing a possessive hand on Derrick's chest.

"Man, have you done a job on her." Cam feigned disgust.

"It's called love," Derrick corrected, placing a brief kiss on her lips. "Right, baby?"

"Right." She willed her fluttering heart to be still.

"Now that you see how devoted she is to me, will you stop trying to steal my fiancée?"

"No promises." Cam displayed a devilish grin.

"Will you two excuse me?" Alesha said.

She rose, as did her dinner companions, and walked in the direction of the ladies' room. She definitely needed a moment to compose herself.

"You and Alesha are very good actors."

"Why do I feel a judgment coming?" Derrick took a sip of his coffee.

"No judgment, just an observation," Cam said with a smile.

"I know I'll regret this, but let's hear it."

"I don't think either of you is completely acting about your feelings."

"That's ridiculous." Derrick took a much-needed swig of his drink.

"Is it?"

Cam's razorlike eyes homed in on Derrick's. Derrick suddenly felt like an insect under a microscope.

"Yes, very. You know why we're getting married."

"Yes, I think *I* know." He leaned closer and added, "But I don't think either of you has a clue."

"Cameron..." Derrick's voice held a warning.

"Shh, here comes your fiancée." Cam laughed at his friend's scowling features.

"Did I miss something?"

Alesha sat beside Derrick once again. The atmosphere was noticeably thicker than when she had left.

"No, I've just made Derrick angry with me again, but

he'll get over it." Cam laughed and received a dark glare from his friend.

"Oh, I see." Alesha carefully glanced from one to the other.

"Alesha, it was a pleasure to finally meet you, but I have to go now." Cam took her hand and brought it to his lips.

"Thank you, Cam. I enjoyed meeting you, too." She smiled genuinely.

"See you tomorrow, Derrick." He continued to grin broadly.

"Goodbye, Cameron."

Derrick's stilted response made his friend laugh.

"See, I told you he was mad at me." He winked at Alesha, who chuckled as he departed.

"What was that all about?" She turned to face her still-scowling fiancé.

"Nothing. Just Cam being Cam." Derrick quickly dismissed a topic of conversation he didn't want to pursue.

"Are you angry with him?"

"Always." Derrick laughed, and she relaxed as his black mood seemed to suddenly dissipate. "You did a wonderful job tonight." He placed his arm alongside the back of the booth, bringing her that much closer.

"Thanks. I was nervous," she admitted with a slight laugh.

"You needn't have been. I told Cam you could do it." He impulsively hugged her shoulders.

"You what?"

She frowned at his words, and pulled slightly out of his embrace. She had been led to believe that Cam didn't know anything about their arrangement.

Chapter 6

"Cam knows." As her frown grew into a glare, he said, "Remember, we're still in public."

She forced a slight smile, though her eyes still shot daggers at him. "You lied to me."

"No. I never said Cam didn't know."

She was annoyed by his truthful reminder. She would have moved farther away, but his arm held her captive.

"But you insinuated as much." Her words were quietly hissed through gritted teeth. "What did you two do? Have a great laugh at my expense?"

"I didn't bring you here tonight to make fun of you."

"Then why?" She resisted an urge to empty the contents of her water glass onto his head.

"Because I needed to know if you could really pull this off with someone who wasn't a friend, a colleague or related to you—someone whose questions you couldn't anticipate, someone who would take you completely off guard. *You* needed to know."

"You still could have told me." Her voice had lost some of its edge as his words sank in.

"It would have undermined the purpose if I had." His logic was inescapable. He studied her closely. "You believe that I wasn't trying to make a fool of you, don't you?"

She studied his earnest expression, and the remainder of her anger dissipated. She might be an idiot, but she did believe him.

"Yes, I believe you." Her body relaxed noticeably.

"Good." He released his breath on a sigh.

"You sound as if you actually care what I think." She fingered the white linen dinner napkin, though her eyes never left his.

"I do."

"Why?" She stopped fiddling with the napkin.

"Do you know what I want to do?"

He didn't answer her question on purpose. It wasn't that he couldn't have, but rather, he wasn't sure she would like his response, or if he cared to hear the truth himself.

"No, what do you want?"

"I want to kiss you." He glanced around the room before returning his full attention to her. "But, unfortunately, we do have quite an audience."

"That's never stopped you before." Her whispered invitation surprised them both.

"No, no, it hasn't." He smiled slightly before his lips captured hers.

It was an earth-shattering kiss. One of his hands cupped her jaw, tilting her head until it lay over his arm as his mouth plundered. Her hand slid up his chest to rest at his nape as she kissed him back. She didn't know how long their mouths feasted, but when he lifted his head, she wished he hadn't stopped. As if reading her thoughts, his mouth settled against hers again and she sighed in pleasure. Her fingers fastened on the back of his head as she held his mouth closer. Long minutes later when he lifted his head again, they were both breathing heavily.

"I'd better get you home." His voice was thick with passion, his eyes dark with longing. She felt the same way.

"Yes." Her voice was barely audible.

His head lowered toward hers again and she waited for another kiss, yet it never came. Instead, he pulled back and summoned the waiter, to pay for their bill.

Neither spoke as they left the restaurant or once they were seated inside the car. Alesha silently contemplated their supposedly purely business alliance, which had quickly evolved into something completely different than she believed either of them had anticipated, yet it seemed that neither was unable or unwilling to arrest its unexpected evolution.

November 29 dawned cold and clear as Alesha and Derrick exchanged their wedding vows. She wore a white, sequined designer gown made especially for her, and her hair was covered by a headpiece and a cathedral veil that trailed behind her when she walked down the aisle. It was a beautiful formal evening affair that rivaled some of the most elegant weddings of celebrities and royalty.

They posed for what must be the thousandth picture of the day, facing each other, bodies pressing close, arms encircling each other as they smiled into the camera. She had to admit that all day they had presented the picture of a deliriously happy couple, very much in love. If she didn't know any better, she herself would swear they were crazy about each other.

Suddenly, the lights dimmed and a space miraculously appeared as people moved to one side in preparation for their private dance. Derrick took her hand and led her slowly onto the dance floor. She gathered the white lace veil closer to her as she went into her husband's waiting arms.

She gratefully buried her face in Derrick's shoulder and dropped the fake smile from her aching countenance. She was able to escape from the peering eyes and cameras for a few blissful minutes. As she moved closer to Derrick, her hand moved from his shoulder to the back of his neck.

"You're doing remarkably well. Don't stop now."

His whispered reminder in her ear annoyed her no end. Why couldn't he be quiet and let her fantasize about this being real?

"Raise your head and give me a kiss for the people like a good wife."

She almost refused—not because she didn't want to, but because she didn't like being ordered to play a part when everything that had transpired today had held special meaning for her. However, she complied and his lips slowly neared hers before closing warmly, firmly over them as they continued to sway slowly to the music. Through her closed eyes, the bright light of camera flashes was evident as more pictures were taken and she heard the hushed sighs of delight as people witnessed the touching scene before them.

Dear Lord, how long did he intend to kiss her? His lips continued to caress and take her breath away, which further delighted the crowd, who whistled and cheered the loving couple before them.

After what seemed like an eternity—and, if she were honest with herself, not an unpleasant one—he lifted his head, yet maintained eye contact with her. She was mesmerized by his gaze, unable to look away.

To onlookers, it must have seemed as if they were totally enamored of each other, impatiently waiting for this elongated celebration to end so they could escape and privately express their love. Of their own accord, her thoughts drifted to the time in the near future when she and Derrick would be completely alone together.

She was at war with herself—part of her wanted more than anything to finally culminate the desire that had been building within her and had gone unquenched since his first touch years ago. Another part of her wished that the reception would go on forever, even though she secretly hated every moment of it. Shamefully, she couldn't decide which part she wanted to win out, and oh, how that bothered her.

The song finally ended, and he led her off the dance floor with his arm still around her waist. She plastered the happy smile on her face once again as they approached her mother and brother.

"I'm so happy for you, dear." Her mother embraced her warmly.

"Thanks, Momma." Alesha smiled as her mother released her. She possessively placed her arm through Derrick's, who covered her hand with his own.

"Derrick, I'm so glad you're a member of our family." Barbara warmly kissed her son-in-law's cheek.

"Thank you, Barbara. You'll never know how much that means to me." He held Alesha close as he smiled at her mother.

Alesha resisted the urge to slap his face. It was one thing lying to all these strangers, but it was another thing doing it to her mother. But was he lying? He seemed genuine enough. She believed he liked her mother and she knew her mother adored him.

Derrick didn't like deceiving this nice lady. She had been nothing but kind to him since they had met, and he genuinely liked her. When she found out the truth, he hoped she would understand. Suddenly, he realized he would hate to lose the special friendship he had developed with Alesha's mother.

That surprised and worried him. He hadn't meant to become attached to Alesha again or anyone in her family. However, that's just what had happened—and in a very short time. What was it about his new wife that captivated him so? He had to be careful not to let himself become any more involved with his wife or her family. Yet, he feared it was already much too late to stop that from occurring.

"How about a glass of punch, Barbara?" Derrick spoke more to quiet his unwanted thoughts than anything else.

"I'd love one, Derrick." Barbara linked her arm through his.

"Excuse us, darling?" He kissed Alesha's lips lightly.

"Of course, sweetheart. I'll be right here." She smiled lovingly at him as he led her mother off.

She was alone with Robert, and she dreaded it. "Robert, don't start," she warned before he could utter a word.

"I don't have anything to say, except I can't believe this is happening." His response was somber.

"It's done. We'll all have to make the best of it."

"Can you do that?" He eyed her closely.

"I have to."

Truthfully, she feared that being Mrs. Derrick Chandler wouldn't be nearly as hard as having to stop being Derrick's wife.

"I'm so sorry."

"I know." She squeezed his hand. "I want you to know that I don't blame you—you know that I understand why you did what you did."

"I know you do." He suddenly grabbed and hugged her close, as if he would never let her go. "If he hurts you…"

"He won't."

She knew without a doubt that Derrick wouldn't harm her physically. However, she was afraid there had already been irreparable damage done to her emotionally. How much more there would be after months of living with him as his wife, she couldn't begin to guess.

"He'd better not."

"Smile." She forced herself to follow her own advice.

He tried, but the smile didn't quite reach his eyes. Her own eyes grew distant as she contemplated her immediate future. Soon, very soon she would have to leave here with her husband—with Derrick. She would have to be alone with him, and she would be expected to give herself to him totally, a prospect that didn't repulse her, but rather unnerved and, dare she think it, excited her.

Today marked the start of new life as Mrs. Derrick Chandler and in a few short hours, she would truly begin her life as his lover. She shivered at the thought. There was no longer any denying to him, and certainly not to herself, that she wanted him physically. In a matter of hours, she would have him and he would, in turn, have all of her with all that implied.

Derrick and Cam stood together watching as Angela, Alesha's maid of honor, and her bridesmaids surrounded Alesha on the other side of the room. Derrick watched his bride with mixed emotions—he had felt strange all day. He had been mesmerized as she had made her stunning entrance at the church. As they had recited their vows, an emotion he dared not name had assailed him. Of course, he knew their marriage was a carefully orchestrated arrangement, but he *really felt married* to her. It was unnerving and exciting. He wondered if she felt the same way.

"Well, you two did it—and very well, I might add." Cam slapped him on the back.

"Did you ever doubt it?" Derrick smiled, grateful for the intrusion on his disturbing thoughts. "Thanks for understanding why I had Robert as my best man."

"No problem. It looked good for the photographers."

"Spoken like a true campaign manager." Derrick chuckled.

"Alesha is a beautiful bride."

"Yes, she is."

Derrick's eyes easily found his wife across the room. She was smiling at something one of her bridesmaids had whispered to her—a beautiful smile, a smile he was sure could light up the world as it lit up his heart.

Cam studied his friend closely as he watched his bride. There was something in his expression that Cam couldn't put a finger on. He had watched the two of them all day, and as he had informed his friend weeks ago, he didn't think either of them was as aloof toward this marriage or each other as they insisted they were.

Derrick, aware of Cam's thoughtful scrutiny turned cool eyes toward his friend. "Don't start."

Cam smiled. "I wasn't going to say a word."

"Oh, yes, you were. But don't."

Derrick's eyes gravitated back to stare at his beautiful bride. Cam's eyes followed Derrick's and his smile widened; though, as his friend had suggested, he remained silent.

All too soon, Alesha sat alone in her dressing room. She gazed at her frightened expression in the mirror. Now that she was alone, she was finally able to let her happy facade fade. Her heart was beating frantically, and she knew if she didn't gain control of herself very soon, she would faint.

She stood and smoothed nervous hands down the front of the pale blue suit she wore. The long jacket almost reached the hem of her just-above-the-knee matching skirt, which had a half-inch slit up the right front side. She brushed her hair until some of the curls had disappeared, but left it loose, though it was brushed away from her face. She slowly sat down again, her wobbly legs unable to support her.

She knew the reason for her apprehension—soon she would be alone with her husband, and would, therefore, put an end to all the imaginings her mind had conjured up about the night that was rapidly approaching. She shuddered visibly as she thought of Derrick and her alone in the most intimate of situations and positions. Despite herself, her heart skipped several beats in…anticipation?

A knock at the door made her jump. Taking a last look at her nervous reflection, she stood, walked over to open the door and found Derrick there.

"Are you ready to go?" His piercing eyes took note of her pale cheeks and troubled eyes.

"Ready as I'll ever be." She placed her arms through the coat he held up for her.

"You look excited."

"What do I have to be excited about?" She pulled away from him, angry that he could read her so easily.

"Nothing yet," he paused suggestively. "But soon."

She gasped. "Are you ready?"

He smiled. "More than ready."

He placed an arm around her slender waist as they walked down the hall. When they reached the top of the spiral staircase, she saw that the single women had gathered at the bottom of the staircase. Alesha turned her back to them and threw the bouquet down. Laughter and shouts of glee reached her as Angela came up with the bouquet, minus a few flowers that had been snatched out along the way as many hands had tried to grab it. Alesha threw a kiss to her best friend, who smiled and held up the bouquet as if she didn't know what to do with it.

She turned toward Derrick, who was smiling wickedly. He slowly slid his hand under the hem of her skirt, raising it slightly to reveal her upper thigh and the pale blue garter that rested there. She braced herself so as not to melt as his hand splayed warmly against her sensitive skin before his fingers began to remove the garter from her thigh. Ever so slowly he pulled the elastic down before finally straightening, eyes gleaming with merriment as he stared into her flushed, embarrassed face. He placed a kiss on her luscious lips before turning and throwing the garter down into the howling men below, right into Cam's outstretched fingers.

"Way to go, Cam!" Derrick's shout caused everyone to burst out in laughter.

"Thanks, bro." Cam's dry tone prompted more laughter from the gathered crowd.

Cam and Angela turned to stare at each other, smiling slightly. He walked over to her slowly, and amid more laughter and wolf calls, placed the garter on her thigh.

"I guess we're next." He smiled into Angela's good-natured eyes.

"That is the tradition." She returned his smile. They both turned to stare as Derrick and Alesha made their way down the stairs.

"I've never been one for traditions, but I think I could make an exception in this case," Cam whispered in her ear.

"Maybe I could, too," she softly responded with her back still toward him, not daring to turn around to face him.

All too quickly, Derrick and Alesha were off amid flying birdseed and well wishes. She caught a glimpse of her mother and brother and blew them both a kiss. Her mother looked ecstatic, while her brother's expression was a mask of melancholy.

They exited the door and ran hand in hand to Derrick's black Jaguar. Once tucked inside, Alesha tried unsuccessfully to quell the nervousness mounting within her. Derrick started the car and it moved smoothly and speedily down the road. She stared out the window until the reception hall was a tiny blur in the distance. Lord help her, she had done it. She was on her way to her new life—a life that, if she was honest with herself, didn't terrify her nearly as much as she had thought it would.

They had been driving for a little over an hour, saying little, each engrossed in their own thoughts. She placed a hand on her nervously churning stomach and closed her eyes, resting her head on the soft leather headrest. She tried to calm her nerves. She wouldn't think about anything for a few minutes. She would just relax and listen to the soft music wafting from the speakers.

Derrick glanced at Alesha's silent profile. Her eyes were closed and she looked tenser than he had ever seen her. He knew she was nervous, but he didn't know what he could do to alleviate that. He had tried to talk and she had been unresponsive. Maybe once they arrived at the house, she would relax, although he silently admitted she would probably get even more tense. He knew she was worried about being alone with him.

He reminded himself again that she had known exactly what she was letting herself in for. He hadn't lied to her or tried to deceive her in any way. He had told her what he had expected, and she had agreed to his terms. Now she would just have to learn to live with her decision.

"Well, here we are."

She jumped nervously at his voice. Opening her eyes, she glanced out the frosty window at the lovely two-story house (which he had called a cottage) as he stopped the car. She remained inside until he walked around and opened the door for her. Taking her hand, he helped her out before leading her inside.

"It's beautiful." She glanced around her apprehensively.

"Thanks." He took her coat and hat, placing them onto a chair in the hallway.

He went back out into the cold night air and returned moments later with their bags, which he sat down in front of the stairs. "Would you like to go to our bedroom and change for dinner?"

Our bedroom, she silently echoed. Oh, the visions those little words fired off in her head. "Yes, thank you."

He nodded and, picking up their bags, started up the stairs. "Follow me."

He ushered her into a spacious room with a huge cherry-oak, king-size bed covered with a black-satin comforter and shams. Much to her relief and dismay, he quickly excused himself after showing her where the bathroom was.

She walked over to the bed and sat down nervously. She fingered the soft comforter, her eyes lingering on the huge bed she and Derrick would be sharing shortly. Visions of the two of them lying there naked, entangled in the soft sheets, tortured and teased her mind. What would his skin feel like against hers? What would it be like to…? She refused to complete that thought, quickly jumped up and almost ran into the bathroom, hoping a hot shower would ease the confusion and maddening sense of anticipation coursing through her veins.

Chapter 7

Approximately forty minutes later, she descended the stairs, wearing an emerald-green, long-sleeved silk dress. Her hair was swept away from her face, though she had left it loose.

Following soft strands of romantic music, she entered the study. Derrick was standing in front of a floor-to-ceiling window, but turned to stare appreciatively at her as she entered.

He was dressed in tan slacks and a burgundy sweater. He had shaven, and seeing his slightly damp hair, she realized that he had showered, too. At least he had not barged in on her. She conceded he was trying to be considerate—for that she was grateful.

At her puzzled gaze, he said, "I used the guest bedroom to change." He slightly stressed the word *change,* making her aware that he would not be using it later when it came time for bed.

She forced herself to walk over to where he stood, stopping inches in front of him. She would have spoken to break the uneasy silence, but she didn't know what to say.

"Did you find everything you needed?" With great difficulty, he resisted the need to touch her.

"Yes." She linked her hands together nervously.

"Dinner is ready, if you are."

"I'm ready." She paused before quickly elaborating, "I'm ready for dinner."

He smiled broadly at her words, but made no further response, ushering her into the dining room where a romantic, candlelit table for two was set. A magnum of champagne was beside the table, and a bouquet of red roses lay beside her plate. She almost laughed out loud as her eyes surveyed the romantic scene before her. If things were different, she would have been pleased—a big part of her was pleased, even now.

He held out her chair for her as she sat down before seating himself opposite her at the small table. He only had to reach his hand out to touch her face—that thought made her breath catch in her throat. To remove her eyes from the disturbing depths of his, she looked at the roses, fingering a soft petal lightly.

"These are beautiful."

"I'm glad you like them."

He wondered why he had an absurd impulse to say something corny, like she was the most beautiful woman he had ever known, or that he was glad she was his wife. "Would you like some champagne?"

"I'd love some." She gratefully accepted, raising her glass as he popped the cork before placing some of the foaming liquid into her glass.

She downed the contents in one gulp before the bubbles had subsided and offered her glass for more. Derrick raised an eyebrow at her actions, but refilled her glass nevertheless. She disposed of that in the same fashion and offered her glass for more. But he shook his head.

"Getting drunk is not going to help anything." He replaced the champagne in its holder.

"I'm not trying to get drunk."

She only wanted to relax—something that seemed impossible to do in his presence.

"Alesha, try to calm down. I'm not going to devour you."

Absurdly, she thought it might not be such a bad thing if he did. She wanted to unleash the passion that had been hinted at every time they had touched. She wanted him, but she was afraid—both of him and of herself.

She managed a half smile. "Derrick, I..."

Unexpectedly, he grabbed her hand, his fingers lightly caressing hers. "It's not as if this is your first time."

She blushed hotly and looked away. How did he expect her to discuss such intimate matters with him? If she told him that he was her first, he wouldn't believe her. He wouldn't believe her because she had led him to believe otherwise, she silently amended.

"Alesha." The soft yet firm way he called her name made her look at him. "I won't rush you."

"I know." Her voice was barely audible as tiny shivers of anticipation raced up her arm at his light, teasing touch.

"Do you?" He spoke so softly she thought she had imagined it.

"Yes." She took a deep breath and then released it slowly. "Maybe if I had a few days to..."

"No, Alesha, there will be no days, weeks or months," he quickly yet gently interrupted, fingers stilling their seduction of her wrist. "I mean to make love to you tonight."

She snatched her hand away from his. "Do you have to talk so bluntly?"

He sat back in his chair and poured himself a glass of

champagne. Taking a sip he reminded, "We are husband and wife."

"I know, but it's so…new…" Her voice trailed off. She suddenly longed for some more champagne—a lot more.

"You want me, don't you?"

His question made her eyes grow to twice their normal size. She was glad she didn't have any champagne in her glass to drink. She would have choked on it.

"How can you ask me such a thing?" She brought a hand to her suddenly constricted throat.

"It's obvious." He smiled slightly at her distress. "That bothers you, doesn't it?"

"What do you expect? Ours is not exactly a normal marriage, is it?" She didn't deny or confirm his words. "Can't you try to be more patient?"

"I am, and I have been." His response was calm. "I could have already taken you while we were engaged. However, I gave you time to adjust."

"Don't say that!" She fidgeted uncomfortably in her seat as red stained her cheeks.

"Say what?" He smiled slightly, knowing to what she alluded.

"You know what." She ran her tongue across her dry lips and his eyes watched her every movement. "It sounds so, so…animalistic." He laughed heartily at her words, and that was her undoing. "Damn you. Don't be amused by me!"

"It's hard not to be." He wiped the tears of merriment from his eyes. *"Animalistic?"* he echoed, still smiling. Then, seriously, he said, "You don't know what animalistic is…" He paused for emphasis before adding, "yet."

She stood abruptly, food forgotten. "I'm really not very hungry. I'd like to…" She stopped herself, eyes widening in shock at what she had been about to say.

He also stood. "You'd like to what?" He smiled wickedly.

"Go to bed?" He'd correctly interpreted what she had been about to say.

"No, I wasn't going to say that, I..." Her voice trailed off as her heart leaped in her throat.

"Let's both go to bed." He took her hand and nearly dragged her up the stairs, not stopping until they reached their bedroom.

Once inside, he started to pull her into his arms. "Wait!" She placed hands on his chest to ward him off. Things were moving too fast—much too fast. "I—I have to change."

"Why? You won't wear it for long." He pulled her body closer again.

"Please, please, Derrick." Her hands on his chest warded him off.

He looked at the nervous expression on her face and he knew she needed a little more time. "All right, but don't take too long."

"I won't." She picked up her overnight case before almost running to the bathroom, shutting the door behind her and locking it.

She leaned weakly against the door. She tried to quiet the frantic thudding of her heart as she opened her overnight bag. She should be angry and appalled that in a few minutes she would be expected to make love to Derrick, but she wasn't. If she were honest with herself, she was expectant. She was also nervous, excited and confused.

Damn Derrick's undeniable effect on her and damn Robert, too, for getting her into this mess! With a sigh of resignation, she glanced into her overnight bag and saw a white silky negligee with matching robe, which left nothing to the imagination.

"Oh, Mother!"

How could her mom have done this to her? She must have taken out her flannel gown and replaced it with this one. She couldn't go out there wearing this! She rummaged further into her luggage and saw other negligees, all just as revealing. Carefully inspecting the diaphanous, flimsy creation in her hands, she admitted it was a knockout. The long gown was made of several layers of the sheerest chiffon she had ever seen, and the bodice and waist consisted of lace, which would allow tantalizing glimpses of her skin to peek out. The single-layer chiffon robe might as well be nonexistent for all that it covered. Well, it was either wear this sexy creation or nothing, so she quickly donned the ensemble and almost fainted when she saw how little it actually hid.

After several minutes of deep breathing, which did nothing to calm her nerves, Alesha went to the door and grabbed the doorknob. She willed herself to calm down. She was married now, and on the other side of the door, her husband waited for her. Though their marriage was the result of a distasteful arrangement, she silently admitted that their mutual desire for each other was very real—as real as real could get. Soon she would know the culmination of the scandalous kisses they had shared. At that thought, she trembled visibly and, gathering the folds of the robe closer to her in one hand, she opened the door with the other and slowly exited the bathroom.

The only light in the bedroom came from candles beside the bed, which had been turned down. Derrick stood on the opposite side of the room, though he faced her as she entered. He was dressed in a black robe.

Alesha stopped just outside the bathroom. He couldn't believe the tremendous surge of hunger he felt just staring at her luscious body in that sexy gown. In fact, he couldn't believe she had packed such a piece of lingerie, but he was glad she had.

She was the most beautiful woman he had ever seen. He wanted her as he had wanted no other. He couldn't believe that finally she was going to be completely his. Slowly, purposefully, he walked toward her, expecting her to flee at any moment. Yet she remained rooted to the spot, nervous, expectant eyes making tentative contact with his. The pulse at the base of her neck was beating rapidly and he longed to place his lips there. He stopped mere inches away.

"*Beautiful* is too mild a word to describe how you look."

He reached out his hands and lightly cupped her warm cheeks. A shudder passed through her at his touch. He took her breath away for he was staring at her as if she were the most important person in the world. If she didn't know any better, she would think he was madly in love with her.

"Alesha, we've waited a long time for this."

She shook her head in agreement. "I know, but…" She paused, unable and unwilling to try to verbalize her topsy-turvy feelings as far as he was concerned.

"But what?" His hands dropped to her shoulders, lightly massaging her tense flesh.

"I—I don't know…" Her voice trailed off again.

"You don't have to know anything." His strong hands made soothing circles on her overheated skin. "Except that I want you."

"Do you?" His sincere words helped quiet some of the butterflies intent on making mincemeat out of her stomach lining.

"Yes, I do. Very much." The ease of his confession left little doubt as to its veracity. "Do you believe me?" He had always wanted her, and finally she was going to be his.

"Yes." She sighed the word.

"And you want me."

She gasped lightly as his fingers drew the robe from her shoulders and let it fall in a soft heap at her feet. His eyes mesmerized her.

"I…" She couldn't bring herself to admit that, too.

"It's all right. I know."

That voice of his was turning her bones to mush. His hands slid down her bare, silky arms and back up again several times, causing her breathing to increase expectantly.

"All right."

The arms on her shoulders drew her closer until their bodies were touching lightly. His eyes never left hers. Though she made no effort to move out of his arms, he knew she was still apprehensive. He wanted to replace her anxiety with passion and longing—emotions he knew were smoldering just beneath the surface.

He slowly lowered his lips to hers, and placed a light kiss on her quivering mouth. His lips then trailed down her cheek to her earlobe, where he gently bit into her flesh before moving to the side of her neck, his teeth and tongue lingering there, reverently tasting her silky, delicately perfumed skin.

Something strange was happening to her as he continued his pleasing caresses. She felt a little breathless as overpowering feelings began building within her body. After several long, pleasing minutes, his mouth trailed down her shoulder, his hands sliding the thin straps of her gown out of the way, down her arms, as his lips explored her tremulous skin. She closed her eyes, allowing herself to enjoy the extraordinary sensations engulfing her body at his every touch.

His lips moved to her other shoulder, teeth gently scraping across her skin, sending shivers of delight up and down her spine. The hands that had been resting on his muscled arms tightened slightly as he trailed his hot tongue from her neck to her cheek, slowly outlining her tender lower lip. Her eyes were half closed as wonderful tremors coursed through her.

His hands moved from her shoulders to her lower back, to rest intimately on her buttocks, pulling her closer to his masculine physique. She was suddenly aware of every muscle in his body as she was molded to his hard frame. The ache in the pit of her stomach increased almost unbearably.

His lips played lightly with hers, rubbing, nipping softly and then pulling away again, but refusing to end the sweet torture he was subjecting her to. She unashamedly longed to feel his mouth close warmly and decisively over her own. What was he doing to her? This question ran through her dazed mind while she could still think, before, finally, she received what she wanted when his strong mouth hotly engulfed hers.

Like a starving man feasting, his lips hungrily wandered over hers, his marauding tongue sliding beneath the quickly conquered barrier of her white teeth to find and engage in a slow, thorough dance of rising passion with hers. She felt light-headed, overwhelmed with sensation and completely wanted and desired. They had shared many kisses since their engagement, but this was different because she knew, this time, there would be no stopping, interruptions or turning back, and she was absurdly pleased about that. After an eternity of waiting, she was about to fully experience Derrick's lovemaking, and she wanted that more than she had ever wanted anything.

Her arms on his shoulders encircled his neck of their own will. Her fingers tentatively massaged his nape. At her response, his mouth hardened, crushing her lips beneath the pressure his exerted as he intimately deepened the kiss, voraciously ravaging her sweet mouth.

She moaned in pleasure, on fire and wanting—what, she didn't know. Vaguely, she felt him slide the gown from her overheated body and realized she was standing naked in his arms, but she didn't care. All that mattered was that he not stop kissing her—ever. She clung to him unashamedly as he thirstily drank again and again from her luscious lips.

As he lifted her easily, she then felt the cool, satiny softness of the sheets beneath her back. She vaguely realized
they were both lying on the bed. Derrick still wore his robe
and the textured material brushed against her overly sensitive flesh.

He reluctantly released her enticing lips and withdrew
from her slightly to stare at her face. She was so beautiful, and he wanted her so much, yet he couldn't rush her or
himself. After years of waiting, he was determined that she
would enjoy this as much as he was going to. She stared at
him through half-closed, aroused eyes, a thousand questions
in her expression.

He smiled slightly and, propping himself up on one
elbow, trailed one hand from her collarbone to the tip of a
firm, ripe breast, slowly drawing circles around her chocolate nipple. He smiled as she audibly gasped in pleasure.
His smile deepened and his traveling fingers became more
ardent as he continued his masterful manipulations of her
willing flesh.

When his thumb and forefinger encircled her hard nipple,
she moaned aloud, unable and unwilling to stop herself. His
mouth slowly lowered to taste the flesh his hand had just
caressed. She waited for what seemed like hours until his
hot, warm, rough tongue licked across her nipple and she
groaned louder, closing her eyes against the sweet pain rapidly invading her body.

His hand trailed down her flat, trembling stomach, his
palm rubbing against her skin as his mouth enclosed her
breast. He pulled at her skin, softly at first, but then with increasing intensity. She felt as if she would die at any second
from the exquisite torture he was inflicting on her.

Her hands drifted to the back of his head, holding him
closer to her flesh. When he bit into her skin, she simultaneously bit her lip to hold back the scream that wanted so

desperately to escape from her mouth, while her hands held him closer still. After several agonizingly wonderful seconds, his hot roving mouth moved to repeat the process on her other breast. She stopped trying to hide her pleasure at his touch and passionate moans of pleasure escaped from her lips.

Her fingers ran up and down his head, holding him closer still, and the hand on her stomach moved to trail across one of her silky inner thighs, before moving to touch her more intimately than anyone ever had, and she was suddenly lost in a savage, merciless storm.

Raising his head, he watched the play of emotions that crossed her face as he did things to her she had only dreamed of. Her body shuddered uncontrollably and her hoarse screams of pleasure filled the room as he continued his mind-shattering stroking of her pliant body. He wanted her to forget every other man she had ever been with. His would be the face she saw, his the name she uttered. She would cling to his body and give herself to him completely.

He fought the urge to plunge into her. She was so wet, so warm, so inviting. His teeth bit into her nipple again and she arched against him, her hips moving rhythmically against his skillful fingers as he continued to assail her with passion.

Why hadn't someone warned her that she would feel this way as his expert hands stroked her novice body? She had never imagined that anything could feel so marvelous! It couldn't get any better than this, could it? Her question was answered emphatically yes with each subsequent devastating caress Derrick bestowed on her. She clung to him weakly, unabashedly begging for release of the sweet tension coiling inside her. She didn't think she could take much more, but each touch proved her wrong.

Derrick shrugged out of his robe and immediately covered her soft, welcoming body with his own. She gasped at the intimate contact, feeling every hard, masculine inch of him against her. His lips covered hers again and again. Her arms entwined around his neck before moving to slide down his powerful shoulders and his muscled back, enjoying the rough texture of his flesh against the satiny softness of her own. Her body begged him to end the wonderful torment he had stirred up within her.

He tore his mouth away from hers to bury it in the soft hollow of her neck as he rasped her name over and over again before lifting his head to stare at her face—highly aroused, yet somewhat troubled. She opened her eyes slightly within a few seconds and stared at him questioningly. He wanted to bury himself in her, he wanted to lose himself in her, and he was going to do just that and more.

His eyes burned her with their intensity, his body lighting an answering inferno within her own as one of his muscled legs slipped between her satiny thighs. She gasped at the intimacy and her heavy eyelids began to droop.

"Alesha, just enjoy it—enjoy us," he urged. "Just feel," he added as he devastated her in a kiss that seared her to her very being.

His limbs entangled closely with hers. Intent on savoring each second, he slowly, inch by inch, merged their bodies into one. She felt engulfed by heat and slight pain as he slowly filled her—he was hot, hard and throbbing. He then glanced down at her, shock evident in his expression.

"Alesha?"

He couldn't comprehend what his mind and her body was telling him. She was a virgin! How could she be a virgin? He continued to stare into her shimmering eyes. He started to withdraw, but she was so soft, so warm and fluid that he couldn't bring himself to leave her, so he pressed deeper. He lay motionless for a few moments, and when she began to whimper against his hot mouth, and the hands on his back began to caress him, only then did he begin to move—slowly at first, yet urgently.

Her body shuddered beneath his as momentary pain quickly gave way to immense pleasure. Hot molten lava flowing through her veins at his every erotic, pleasurable touch. Sensations she hadn't dared to imagine erupted from the core of her being as Derrick opened her eyes to a wondrous desire whose existence she had never suspected.

His powerful body continued to move frantically against hers. She instinctively arched to get closer to him. He groaned at her actions and his hands moved down her sides to rest on her hips, pressing her closer still, wrapping one of her slender legs around his waist as their passion rose higher and higher still, threatening to consume them both with its ferocious intensity.

Many times, she had dreamed of this moment—what it would feel like to make love to Derrick completely and totally—yet this surpassed all her expectations. Forgotten was the fact that she had once driven him away, as was the fact that she had married him only to save her brother. Now, right now, he was the only person who could give her the release she so desperately craved. He was the only one who could bring her dormant body to glorious, vibrant life.

They floated high, higher still on tenuous waves of life-affirming passion. When the moment of culmination came, she cried out into his mouth and he into hers. Her eyes, filled with wonder, flew open to stare into the blazing depths of his. Their bodies began to shake uncontrollably as the throes of their passion blinded them to everything except the unparalleled bliss they experienced in each other's arms as they drifted slowly into a miraculous abyss of complete and total fulfillment.

Some time later, he marshaled enough energy to remove

his body from hers. They lay breast to breast on their sides, his hand resting on her waist.

"Did I hurt you?" His warm breath vibrated against her ear.

"No." Her single-word response was muffled as she hid her face in his hair-covered chest, inhaling the heady male scent of him, which intoxicated her.

On the contrary, she silently amended. He had made her feel wonderful, vibrant and alive. She had wantonly enjoyed his thorough possession of her, as she had never enjoyed anything else in her life. She had clung to him, whimpering, begging for his kisses and caresses. She had found rapture in his arms beyond belief. Had he known? Of course, he must have. Why didn't that bother her? She had responded shamelessly to him and her body felt completely fulfilled against his, as if this was where she was meant to be.

Out of duty to some absurd unwritten rule, she tried to roll away from him, but was glad when he wouldn't let her go. His strong arms held her close to his masculine form, a body that had moments before given her the greatest gratification she had ever imagined. She stayed where she was, where she wanted to be, close to her husband.

Derrick knew she wanted some time to rationalize what had just happened between them, and he knew that no matter how hard she tried, she wouldn't be able to. She would never be able to discount what they had just shared—neither would he. She felt so good lying in his arms, her soft body yielding against his.

She was so inexperienced, but she had aroused him as no other woman ever had. He was her first lover, the first one to awaken her to the desires of her own sumptuous body. Given what had happened two years ago, he didn't understand how that could be. However, it was undeniably true—Alesha had been a virgin. Why had she lied to him about that?

Slowly, he ran his hands down her slender, silky back, pressing her closer, feeling her shudder against him. He wanted her again and again. Yet he resisted temptation for the moment—they needed to talk. He needed some long-overdue answers. He lowered his head to look at her and she tried to bury her face into his chest. His hand moved under her chin, forcing her to meet his gaze.

"Look at me."

When she complied, he placed a lingering kiss on her tempting lips, but pulled away before things got out of hand. Her beautiful face was marred with uneasiness and he knew she was aware of the questions swirling through his mind.

"Derrick…"

"Alesha, why didn't you tell me you were a virgin?"

He asked the question she dreaded but expected. How in the world should she respond?

"I don't want to talk about it." She lowered her head onto his chest to escape his piercing gaze.

"We have to talk about it." A firm hand under her chin lifted her eyes to meet his darkening ones. "Why did you lie to me two years ago?"

"Derrick, please. I can't talk about this now—not now." Her eyes begged him to understand what he couldn't possibly.

"I don't know what game you're playing…" His voice was understandably upset.

"It's not a game," she quickly contradicted. It hurt her to have him think of her as deceptive when she was merely confused.

"Then, what?" He studied her with simmering anger evident in his expression. "Why the pretense?"

She longed to tell him everything, but what had once seemed so clear and logical now seemed silly and juvenile. She could no longer justify to herself her reasons for hurting him two years ago and for denying them the bliss they had just shared. How could she justify it to him?

All she wanted was to snuggle in his arms, close her eyes and enjoy being with him, but she couldn't. She felt too ashamed and too confused to do that, and she couldn't face any more of his justifiable anger and questions, either.

"Please, just leave me alone."

Avoiding his eyes, she turned away from him again. This time, he allowed her to break free from his embrace. She immediately missed his warm hard body and felt completely bereft.

He looked at her bare back oddly and started to touch her, but stopped himself. Damn her, she owed him an explanation, and he wanted one! He reached out a hand to turn her around to face his righteous anger, but stopped himself. He needed to calm down. If they spoke now, he would say things out of anger he would regret later. Unable to help himself, he swore out loud and she jumped at the sound, though she made no move to face him again. He lay back against the pillows and placed a hand on his head in disbelief. Given the sweet rapture they had just shared, how ludicrous that they were now acting like complete strangers. Damn her, and damn himself for still wanting her with every breath he took!

She pulled the satin sheet closer about her and her body tingled as the soft material brushed against her flesh, made overly sensitive by Derrick's hands, mouth and body. Even now, she unabashedly wanted him. Her body ached for his, but did he still want her?

Chapter 8

Hours later, she was still lying with her back to him as far to her side of the bed as possible—not wanting any incidental contact of their bodies to spark any smoldering flames in either of them. She had never been so uncomfortable in her life, afraid almost to breathe for fear that he would know she was awake and once again ask questions she didn't know how to answer.

She wanted him as desperately as she had hours ago. She longed to feel his strong arms around her, but she couldn't face the anger or the questions that she knew would still be reflected in his eyes when he looked at her. What was she going to do now? How was she going to continue in this marriage and face his inquiries about her past behavior on a daily basis?

What she silently feared and longed for occurred when he shifted suddenly, placing a strong arm around her waist, pulling her back against his warm, hard body. The fingers of one of his hands splayed across her stomach as his lips caressed the side of her neck and shoulder.

The hand on her stomach moved up slowly, massaging her pliant flesh to cup a full breast. He stroked her skin as his warm lips explored the soft skin of her neck, shoulder and back.

She closed her eyes as familiar sensations began to overwhelm her. When one of his legs slid between hers, she moaned with pleasure. His wandering fingers slid languidly back down her quaking body to her stomach and lower, moving to gently explore her pulsing depths, pushing deeply inside her again and again, eliciting ecstasy within her.

"Oh, God," she whispered as he continued his devastating caresses.

She felt him smile against her shoulder and his teeth bit gently into her flesh. She arched back against him and one of her hands covered his as his fingers drove her crazy with longing.

His hands slowly turned her until she was lying on her back and his mouth captured hers in a singeing, greedy kiss, which stole her labored breath away. His body covered hers, his hands entangling themselves in her hair as he pulled her mouth closer to his. Her hands clung weakly to his shoulders before urgently moving down his back to rest on his hips as his mouth continued to ravage hers again and again. She wanted him so much it hurt.

He never said a word, yet his body spoke volumes. She didn't doubt he was still angry at her, but he also still wanted her. Perhaps that would be enough for now.

Her body melted against his. She willingly lifted her hips as he plunged forcefully into her waiting void—filling her completely. She closed her eyes and traveled with him to that wonderful place he had carried her to before, where nothing mattered except the two of them and their passion for each other.

He manipulated her, controlled her, sent her into such a fever pitch, she thought she would literally burst from the mind-bending pleasure she felt. She didn't, though, but rather yearned for more. His lips slid from hers to rest in the hollow of her neck, opening moistly over the pulse beating erratically there, his teeth scraping over her skin. His body continued to masterfully caress hers.

Hoarse moans of pleasure escaped from her lips. Her eyes were tightly shut as her body began to shudder, softly at first, but with increasing intensity, as did his. Her fingers stroked his rippling back as she pressed closer to the man who was now her husband and her lover. His body pressed hers into the soft mattress as they soared higher and higher on waves of desire. Once again, she obtained a glimpse of heaven in her husband's arms.

She slowly awakened the next morning, stretching languidly against the unfamiliar feel of satin on her naked skin. Her hair covered her eyes, and she pushed it away with an impatient hand.

She glanced around the unfamiliar room. Why was her body so sore? Where was she? These and many other questions tumbled through her dazed mind, until she suddenly remembered. Slowly, she turned to look toward the side of the bed on which Derrick had lain last night but, to her relief—and dismay—he was gone.

She slowly brought a trembling hand to her mouth as she remembered him turning to her again in the night. More importantly, she remembered her response to him. She had to admit that he had been a wonderful, considerate and passionate lover. In fact, he had been everything she had ever fantasized about and more.

Sighing, she slid out of bed, taking the sheet with her. She walked by her robe and gown, which Derrick had strewn carelessly on the floor. As she bent to pick them up before placing them on a chair, her mind again drifted toward last night and the wonderful discovery it had held.

She entered the bathroom and dropped the sheet. Her mouth dropped open as she caught a glimpse of herself in the full mirror and stopped in shock. Was this her? Her face looked different, maturer. Her lips were slightly swollen from the numerous ardent kisses Derrick had placed there. Her breasts looked full and tender from his hands and mouth. Hot color flooded her cheeks as she beheld the evidence of Derrick's conquest of her body. She was a woman now—she was Derrick's woman. Derrick, her husband, a man who baffled and inflamed her mind, body and soul.

Turning away from the disturbing picture she presented, she walked over and turned the shower on full blast. Stepping under the steaming spray, she grabbed a bar of soap and slowly foamed her still-tingling body. Where was Derrick? What would she say to him when she saw him? She still had no satisfactory answers to his questions.

Long minutes later, she stepped out of the shower, her skin squeaky-clean. She wrapped a towel, sarong-style, around her wet hair and grabbed a bath sheet to place over her body. Before she could accomplish that task, however, the door burst opened and Derrick appeared casually dressed in jeans and a white sweater—looking very handsome and desirable.

She gasped at his intrusion and tried to pull the towel in front of her. However, his strong hands stopped her. Taking the plush material from her fingers, he slowly proceeded to thoroughly dry every inch of her.

He slid the towel slowly down her shoulders and arms. Then he drew the material across her collarbone and sensuously across her swollen breasts, which hardened at the contact of his toweled hands. A soft sigh escaped from her lips as she waited for him to go further.

His eyes moved from her aroused face to follow the path of his hands as they continued their descent down her satiny skin, moving to brush across her flat stomach, shapely hips, thighs and feet before he slowly walked behind her and dried her back, buttocks and legs.

Returning to stand in front her, he dropped to his knees, his toweled hands moving to her inner thighs with increasing urgency, staying there longer than was necessary before he totally discarded the towel and replaced it with his fingers. Her knees went weak, and she swayed until her back gratefully encountered a nearby wall.

Her breathing was ragged and her fingers flexed on his broad shoulders to steady herself as his fingers continued their manipulation of her fevered body. When his mouth replaced his fingers, she cried out at the multitude of new, wonderful feelings that assaulted her tremulous body.

His hot tongue delved deeply into her moist, pulsing recesses, darting, twisting, turning, retracting and seeking again and again—first slowly, then faster and faster. He drove her to the brink of ecstasy and back. All the while, she longed for more, much more.

Her body shook convulsively. She closed her eyes tightly and her head rolled from side to side as he continued his devastating exploration of her all-too-willing flesh. A thousand tiny, brilliant stars exploded behind her closed eyes as his mouth and lips slowly trailed back up her body to stare at her face, clouded by passion, silently pleading with him for a release only he could give. He removed the towel from her wet hair, fingers sliding through the damp tresses.

She was trembling as he reverently stared at her naked form, his eyes burning her with their intensity. She almos pleaded with him to make love to her. She didn't have to verbalize her desire—he knew what she wanted, and he wanted the same thing.

He reached out and lightly brushed her nipple, which hardened automatically at his now-familiar touch. He smiled slightly as he drew her into his arms and placed a passionate, all-consuming kiss onto her quivering lips. Despite her resolve not to, she welcomed his erotic kisses as much as she had his intimate caresses.

His hands pulled her slightly away from the wall to roam down her bare back, pressing her closer. He suggestively rubbed his hips against hers and she whimpered against his mouth. Her arms encircled his neck and she ardently returned his kisses. Feelings—similar to those that had surfaced last night, yet somehow stronger—began to overwhelm her, nearly crippling her. God help her, she wanted him with every painful breath she took.

His mouth plundered hers for several wonderful minutes. She began to moan against his lips, opening her mouth wider beneath his, wishing he would stop this sweet, sweet torture and satisfy them both.

She was quivering uncontrollably as his lips slid from hers and he slowly took a full breast into his hot mouth. His hands moved to her round buttocks, holding her closer against his intense need as he continued to taste her overheated skin.

He hadn't meant for this to happen. He had wanted to catch her off guard and demand answers to questions she had evaded last night. However, one look at her luscious body and all rational thought had fled—just as it had last night. He didn't know why, despite her obvious deceit, but she excited him and made him feel more alive than he ever had.

Her fingers held his head closer to her and his teeth bit

into her nipple, causing her to gasp out aloud. His hands lightly caressed her sides before moving to her back as he lifted his head to again ravage her mouth, simultaneously sliding his hands up to rest on her lower back. Her fingers held his head fast as their wild, unexpected, intensely satisfying encounter proceeded.

Suddenly, he pulled his mouth away from the intoxicating depths of hers and, disengaging her hands from his head, placed them on his chest instead. She opened passion-glazed eyes to stare longingly at him, not wanting him to stop—ever.

"Undress me."

His soft, urgent command made its way through the foggy recesses of her mind. She gasped audibly, but her fingers moved to obey, sliding beneath the sweater he wore, lightly touching his muscled, hairy chest, making him suck in his breath sharply. Her fingers lightly stroked his chest before she pulled the garment up and over his head, throwing it in a careless heap on the floor. Fascinated eyes watched as her fingers slowly smoothed over his powerful shoulders to his arms, enjoying every nuance of the journey.

"Now my pants." His words were whispered against her mouth, his tongue urgently reaching between her lips to touch hers.

His hands guided her to the snap of his jeans, helping her unfasten it. Her hands would have moved away, and he knew it. So his own hand captured one of hers, slipping it beneath the material to encounter his burning flesh.

She gasped, her eyes staring into his hypnotic gaze. She saw the blatant desire written in his eyes and knew it mirrored her own. At his insistence, she touched him fleetingly before his fingers urged her to engulf him totally.

Her breathing was now ragged, as was his. She wanted to move her hand away, yet wanted to continue her forbidden exploration of his marvelous masculine form. He filled her hand as she longed for him to fill her body. Again his lips closed over hers hotly, eyes blazing bright before hers closed against the intense brilliance.

Somehow, his jeans were discarded and he grabbed her buttocks, lifting her slightly before he entered her easily. Her legs automatically wrapped themselves around his waist as he pressed her against the cool, white-tile wall with his body, frantically.

She clung to him wildly, her mouth mating recklessly with his. As she raked her nails down his rippling back, she vaguely wondered who this ravenous stranger was. It couldn't be her! Just as soon as the thought entered her mind, it left, as Derrick's masterful body continued to bombard hers, driving all rational reasoning from her mind. Agonizing pleasure built inside her until she thought she would explode from the force rapidly mounting to near bursting.

"You're so sweet—so sweet," he murmured against her mouth, his breath erotically intermingling with hers before engulfing her lips once again.

Her hands moved up and down his muscled back, her nails digging into his rippling flesh. The legs around his waist tightened, pulling him closer to her as his writhing body continued to both soothe and excite hers. After several long, agonizing moments, she hoarsely screamed into his mouth as he fulfilled her totally. His mouth took her screams, cries and whimpers as their bodies fiercely gave and took from each other.

She suddenly opened her eyes, staring into the fiery depths of his as their passion reached the wonderful moment of gratification. In that instant, she knew, as she was sure he did also, that her body belonged to him. There was no way she could deny that. However, she must take special care to ensure that her heart didn't follow suit. Yet she silently admitted it was already much too late for that.

Later, about 2:00 p.m., they walked side by side dressed alike in jeans, sweaters and leather jackets. Despite herself, Alesha had to admit she was having a good time with her husband. It was a cloudy, cold November day with the temperature in the forties. She sniffed appreciatively as different pleasant fragrances assailed her overactive senses.

Much to her surprise, Derrick made no attempt to question her about the revelations of last night, but rather showed her particular points of interest, and what she had seen of the grounds on which his house sat was lovely. They stopped to sit on a cobblestone bench in front of a babbling brook.

She unexpectedly asked, "Why have you never married?"

Did she imagine it or did a shadow fall over his face at her query? She didn't know what had made her ask that question, or why she waited with baited breath for his response.

He stood and walked to stare into the water with his back to her. She waited for him to speak.

"I'm sorry if that was too personal."

He threw a rock into the pond and turned to face her. "I was married briefly after we broke up."

Her mouth dropped open in shock. She couldn't help it, nor could she seem to force it to close again. She waited silently for him to continue, his demeanor telling her there was much more to the story.

"Nothing to say?"

His voice was bitter, and though he still had his back to her, she imagined his eyes matched his suddenly dark mood.

"I—I don't know what to say."

He smiled slightly without humor. "No questions?"

She had a thousand, but she didn't dare ask any of them. Who had he married? Had he loved her? How soon after their breakup had he married her? When and why had they divorced? Did they keep in touch? Did she live in Washington?

"Do you want to tell me about it?"

She stood and walked over to him. She watched, intrigued, as a multitude of emotions, none of which she could name, crossed his face. He treated her to a piercing, unnerving stare.

"There's nothing to tell. To make a short story even shorter, after too much liquor, I married her in Vegas on the spur of the moment—it was the worst mistake of my life. We didn't know each other, but it soon became apparent that we wanted different things out of life, so we quickly divorced." He succinctly, coldly summed up the worst period of his life.

"I'm sorry." Even to her own ears, her apology sounded pathetic.

"Why are you sorry, Alesha?" He walked closer to her. "Because you know your actions drove me to it?"

"No." She shook her head and stood abruptly. "I didn't know."

"Oh, but you did." He grabbed her arm and pulled her close. "How does that make you feel? Strong? Elated? Happy?"

"No!" She tried to pull her arm free, but he wouldn't release her.

"Why? Why did you do it?" He grabbed her other arm and pulled her closer.

"I don't know what you mean."

"The hell you don't!" His grip tightened on her.

"I don't want to talk about this." Her heart was pounding frantically—surely he must hear it.

"Well, I do!" His fingers tightened on her flesh to the point of bruising. "Tell me!"

"I don't know." She shook her head slowly, trying unsuccessfully to free herself.

"Don't give me that, Alesha. Dammit, you owe me the truth!"

She had never seen him this angry, and she hoped she never would again.

"I don't..." The pure rage in his eyes halted her words.

"Tell me!" He shook her slightly.

"You frightened me!" she blurted out and almost fell as he suddenly released her.

"Frightened you?" He stood and looked as if she had struck him.

"Yes." She rubbed her throbbing arms.

"How?" That one word was spoken tightly and contained a multitude of anger and pain.

She moistened her lips and met his incredulous gaze. "We had only known each other for a short time, yet what I felt for you, what I sensed you felt for me, was so intense. You consumed my every waking and sleeping thought. I was saturated with you. I—I just couldn't handle it anymore."

"So you let me believe you had just been passing time with me, playing with my emotions while your lover was out of town?" He shook his head disbelievingly.

"I never meant to do that." Her eyes and voice pleaded with him to believe her.

"But that's what you did!"

"I didn't have a choice."

"You didn't have a choice?" He stared at her as he tried to comprehend her statement.

"You wouldn't leave me alone," she said softly, resuming her seat on the bench. "When you came to my apartment that morning and found Kevin there, one look in your eyes and I knew what you were thinking and I let you think we were lovers because it meant I wouldn't see you again." With difficulty, she recounted the event that had sealed their fate.

"And that's what you wanted?"

It wasn't the chilliness of the day that sent a shiver down her spine, but rather his frigid eyes as he tried to comprehend what she was saying. No, it wasn't what she had wanted at all, but at the time she had thought it was the only option available to her—now she wasn't so sure.

"That's what I needed."

"What you did to both our lives is a crime." His voice was angry, tired and sad.

"I didn't have a choice," she miserably whispered.

"Yes, you did. But for whatever reason, you made the wrong one."

His voice was colder than she had ever heard it and, unfortunately, it was directed toward her. Her actions had made perfect sense to her two years ago, but right now she agreed with his assertion.

"I did what I had to do."

Even as she said the words, she didn't believe them. She deliberately didn't tell him the rest of the story. Why, she didn't know—perhaps because she now doubted her fateful choices, as well.

He opened his mouth to ask one of the thousand questions that he still had, yet closed it again. He turned away as if the sight of her disgusted him and lifted his eyes heavenward. She wanted to say something—anything—but there was nothing she could say, so she remained silent. After long minutes, he turned and gazed at her again.

"Do you know what your rejection taught me?" His voice held an eerie aloofness, which his eyes now echoed.

"What?" She was not sure she really wanted to hear his response.

"That love doesn't exist. It's just a pretty word people

use to get others to do what they want." He smiled without humor.

"You don't mean that."

Her heart contracted at his cold assertion. She had seen a soft and passionate side to him only a few hours ago. The man she knew he was didn't at all fit with the callous picture he was painting for her now.

"I assure you I do."

He stared at her as if he didn't know her, and it was the loneliest she had ever felt in his presence. She forced herself to remain expressionless, but his words hurt—more than she would have thought possible. She understood his feelings and agreed with them. Honestly, she didn't understand her actions herself, anymore—how in the world could she expect him to?

She stood up suddenly. "I'm ready to go back now."

He looked at her strangely before following her as she retraced their steps back to the house. Both were silent as they walked side by side, neither looking at the other, but rather glancing straight ahead contemplatively. When they entered the house, the phone was ringing. Derrick answered it angrily and she stood in the hallway, waiting for him to finish. As he hung up the headset, he told her he had to drive into the city to meet with Cam.

"Do you have to go?"

She should be happy for a respite from his anger, but she wasn't. She hated leaving things as they were between them, even though she had no idea how to repair the damage her lies had inflicted.

"Politics never sleeps." He glanced at her oddly before shrugging and promising, "Don't worry, I'll be back tonight."

"Will you?" Her question was spoken so softly, he thought he had imagined hearing it.

Though he was still upset with her, unable to resist, he placed a hand under her chin and lifted her mouth to his. He kissed her and she returned the kiss, her hands tentatively resting on his shoulders. Though their mouths ate voraciously, he purposefully kept their bodies apart, because if they touched intimately, both knew they wouldn't stop with just a kiss. After long, fulfilling moments, his mouth slowly released hers and he walked to the door.

"I'll see you later."

She sighed heavily. He might hate her for what she had done in the past, but clearly he still wanted her. That was something, wasn't it? Perhaps they could rebuild some semblance of a civil relationship on that. She hoped so, just as she prayed one day he wouldn't look at her with veiled anger and disappointment in his eyes.

Chapter 9

After Derrick left, she wandered around the study before choosing a lengthy murder mystery to read. Before she knew it, she had finished the novel and it was after 6:30 p.m.

She fixed herself a snack then returned to the study, turned on the television and found to her delight that *Casablanca* was on. It was one of her favorite movies. Shortly thereafter, a loud clap of thunder rattled overhead. She walked to the window and opened the blinds. To her amazement, ominous clouds loomed in the sky and streaks of lightning could be seen in the horizon.

The out-of-season storm had blown in without warning. She didn't mind, though—there was nothing she liked better than a good movie and a thunderstorm. Walking back to the television, she turned up the volume to drown out the thunder and sat down again with her feet curled under her. Some minutes later, lightning lit up the room, there was a particularly violent clap of thunder and the TV went black, as did the lamp on the table beside her.

"Oh, no," she moaned, getting up and trying the light switch on the wall, which also refused to illuminate the dark room. "Great! So much for television."

It was almost impossible to see, but she felt her way back to the kitchen and, after searching through several drawers, she found some candles and a box of matches. Lighting several, she walked into the hallway and peered out at the ghostly reflections made by the barren tree limbs when the lightning briefly illuminated the dark. After several seconds, she decided she might as well go upstairs.

Once there, she tried the light switch, just in case, but the room remained in darkness. Placing one candle beside the bed, she lit the other candles Derrick had placed there last night, before taking one with her into the bathroom.

She turned on the water and began to draw a hot bath for herself—hoping the soothing water would help alleviate the jitters, which had suddenly crept up on her.

Once the tub was full, she undressed and sank into the sudsy, steaming water. As she slowly ran her hands over her body, she remembered other hands that had explored her flesh the night before and this morning—Derrick's hands—strong, sensual and pleasing.

Try as she might, and Lord knew she had tried, she could not deny that she wanted him with a single-minded passion that overwhelmed, frightened and yet empowered her. Last night and this morning, she had longed for him to somehow defy the laws of physics and merge their bodies into one. At several points, she had felt as if he had done just that.

Vivid memories of crying out in his arms, clinging to him, and the feel of his naked flesh against hers tormented her. Against her will, her eyes were drawn across the room to one of the white-tile walls. Hot color flooded her cheeks as she remembered how she had shamelessly clung to Derrick this morning as they had made love in this very bathroom.

She grudgingly admitted that he was a fantastic lover—better than all the heroes in the romance novels she had read and in all the love stories she had watched on television or at the movies. With one look from those expressive eyes of his, he could inflame her soul. The slightest touch of his fingers turned her into a mass of putty that begged to be shaped by him. Yes, she was inexperienced, but she somehow knew that no one would ever compare to him.

She sighed audibly as she closed her eyes again, trying without success to make sense out of her ambivalent feelings as far as her husband was concerned. Would he still be angry at her when he returned? No doubt, he would. He had every reason to be. She wondered if she should tell him the rest of the story. Would it make her more sympathetic in his eyes, or more pitiful?

She opened her eyes and slowly stood. Her thoughts wouldn't allow her to relax as she had hoped when she had sunk into the tub. All she seemed capable of doing was thinking of Derrick—wondering where he was, what he was thinking and feeling—and both dreading and looking forward to his return.

Her fingers grabbed a huge black bath sheet and began to dry her body. Automatically, memories of this morning rushed to her mind. She dreamily remembered how his mouth had caressed hers and how his body had… Damn! She forcefully ended that train of thought, angrily threw the towel down and picked up another seductive negligee. This one was black satin and clung to her every curve. In spite of herself, she smiled slightly as she mentally pictured her mother shopping for the revealing nightgowns she had placed into Alesha's luggage.

She shivered as she reentered the bedroom and walked

over to switch on the gas-powered heat before climbing beneath the soft satin sheets and comforter, pulling the cover up to her chin. In a few seconds, she felt completely warm. Her limbs relaxed and her mind was quiet.

All that was missing was... No! She would not say his name again. The rain now mixed with something that sounded like sleet and pelted against the window. She snuggled down against the fluffy pillows beneath her head and began to drift off into sleep. Despite herself, the last thought she had was of Derrick as she wished for his safe return.

Derrick listened impatiently as Cam outlined the remainder of his campaign strategy. Although he hated to admit it, his mind was not on this meeting, but rather on his wife. It was a little after 8:30 p.m. He had been gone longer than he had expected. The snow mixed with sleet worried him, and he hoped she was all right. He had tried to phone her about an hour ago, but the phone lines were down.

"Cam, how much longer are we going to be?" He tapped his fingers against the mahogany tabletop.

"Not much longer, why?"

"Because I'm tired and I want to get back home before the roads get too bad." He sprang off the sofa like a caged tiger and went to stare out the frosty window.

Cam walked over to stand by his friend. "It's not the road conditions that are prompting your sudden lack of interest in your campaign."

Derrick turned to face him, wishing Cam couldn't read him so well. "I am not unconcerned—I'm just tired."

"You're worried about Alesha, aren't you?"

He sighed in annoyance. "Come on, man. Don't start speculating on my relationship with Alesha. We have a business arrangement—that's all!" he insisted with more force than was necessary.

Truthfully, after what had transpired between them last night and this morning, he wasn't sure where they stood, or what he wanted to happen between them. Despite her unexplained lies, all he knew for certain was that he couldn't get her out of his mind, out from under his skin or, he grudgingly admitted, out of his heart.

"If that's true, why are you so worried about her?"

"She's alone in an unfamiliar place with no transportation or phone, and a snowstorm is raging outside. Isn't that enough reason for anyone to be concerned?" Derrick's reasoning was flawless, but he knew it wouldn't fool his best friend.

"Yes."

"But?" Derrick knew he was not going to leave it at that.

"But I think there's more to it than that. I think that, despite yourself, you care for Alesha—that you really see her as your wife, not just as a means to an end."

Hearing his feelings articulated so brilliantly by his friend was unnerving and frustrating. Frustration oozed from every pore.

"Look, Cam, we both know that I tried that once, and I'm not going to make that mistake again."

"Please! As for your first wife, if you want to call her that, she was never right for you. I tried to tell you that. Alesha, however, is another story. But then, you know that, don't you?"

"I'm using her—that's where it begins and ends!" His forceful insistence was more for his own benefit than for Cam's.

"If you say so, Derrick." Cam smiled.

Derrick rolled his eyes. "You believe what you want—you will, anyway. I'm going home." He picked up his jacket and walked to the door.

"Derrick?"

"What?" He turned around impatiently.

"Give Alesha a kiss for me."

"Good night, Cameron," he said, sighing heavily before opening the door.

"Good night, bro." Cam smiled. "Drive carefully."

Derrick made his way home as fast as the lousy weather would permit, which was at a slow crawl, giving him too much time to meditate on Cam's words. Was he beginning to care for Alesha, despite his resolve not to? He knew the answer was yes—he had known that from the moment he had seen her again. He had been strongly attracted to her when they had first met two years ago. He had wanted her since their first touch and had burned for her since their first kiss. Now, after finally making love to her, he couldn't deny that he still cared about her very much.

Why had she lied to him two years ago? He could understand her feelings for him scaring her—hell, he had felt the same way—but why had she allowed him to believe she was involved with someone else? Why not just tell him she felt overwhelmed? It didn't make any sense. There had to be more to it than she was admitting, but what?

He sighed loudly. Why did her motivations matter to him one way or another? He was only using her, wasn't he? As he had told Cam, once he had won the Senate seat, he would let her go and he wouldn't think twice about it. He promised himself that he would. However, he knew he was lying, because the thought of life without Alesha left him chilled to the bone.

Alesha was up nervously pacing the floor when she heard a car drive up around 11:00 p.m. She carefully peered out of the bedroom window and was relieved to see Derrick. She absently noted that the ground was covered with a layer of snow. She ran to the door and prepared to open it, but stopped herself abruptly. What was she doing? She couldn't let him know she had been waiting up for him!

Changing course, she ran over and jumped into the bed, pulling the covers over herself before turning onto her side. Closing her eyes, she began to breathe heavily and evenly as if in a deep sleep. Seconds later, the bedroom door opened and Derrick came in. She felt him peer down at her and forced her breathing to remain even.

He smiled slightly as she pretended to be asleep. He had seen her silhouette at the window, and knew instinctively she had been worried about him; that pleased him immensely. He picked up a candle, humming as he walked into the bathroom, leaving the door partially open. Seconds later, Alesha heard the shower running and Derrick singing.

"Inconsiderate oaf." She sat up slightly. "What if I really was asleep? He could wake up the dead with all of that noise."

When he shut the water off some long minutes later, she quickly resumed her previous position, once again feigning sleep. She heard him walk through the door and, seconds later, the bed shifted beneath his weight as he slid underneath the covers, naked beside her.

She held her breath as he rolled closer to her, placing his arm around her waist, before turning her on her back. She continued to feign sleep, hoping he would take the hint that she didn't want to talk about the past anymore.

"I know you're not asleep. Stop pretending," he said softly, leaning over her.

Knowing it was useless, she slowly opened her eyes to stare at him—his face was only inches away from hers. She resisted the sudden urge to trace the rugged outline of his face with her fingers, followed by her lips. Thankfully, he didn't seem angry, just tired. She prayed he wouldn't bombard her with more questions she had no idea how to answer

"Do you want to talk?" she asked in spite of herself.

"No. No, I don't want to talk."

He lowered his head to hers and she stared at him, mesmerized by his hungry eyes as his lips ever-so-slowly neared hers and touched her mouth. He caressed her lips with butterfly kisses until she was trembling with need. It was all she could do to refrain from begging him to stop this sweet torture and make love to her, and she knew that he knew it, too.

"Cam asked me to give you something."

"What?" Why in the world was he talking about Cam at a time like this?

"This."

His hands threaded themselves into her thick hair and lifted her head slightly off the pillows, forging his lips with hers. He kissed her in a way that should have been illegal and probably was. There was no way she could fail to respond to the sensual assault, and she offered no resistance. Rather, she capitulated without thought or question.

Her lips melted against the incinerating heat of his, her tongue responding to the insistent pressure of his. He laid her head back on the pillows and his body half covered hers as he continued to devastate her with his mouth.

His hands moved to her shoulders, easing the thin straps of her gown down as his fingers explored her creamy, burning flesh. His lips slid from her mouth to her chin, gently biting into her burning skin before moving down her silky throat to rest in the valley between her full breasts.

Her breathing increased rapidly at his touch, and a familiar ache began slowly spreading through her abdomen at his increasingly ardent caresses. He pulled the gown down to reveal her breasts and blew his warm breath onto one of her nipples, which stiffened in response. She moaned as he pulled her swollen flesh into his mouth—his tongue and teeth ravaging her softly scented skin.

His wandering hands moved to pull the gown farther down her quivering body, from her stomach to her hips, as he continued to devour her with increasingly ardent caresses. Her hands moved to his shoulders, pressing closer to his body as he continued to ignite her with his fiery touch.

She began to moan, wantonly craving his total possession. She clung to him openly, her own hands exploring his rippling back, pressing him tightly against her throbbing body. At times his caresses hurt, at others they soothed—yet, always they pleased and inflamed.

He raised his head to lightly touch his lips to hers, and she dazedly realized that she no longer wore her gown. Their bare, heated bodies now touched intimately. She waited for his kiss, and when it didn't materialize, she opened her glowing eyes to encounter the smiling yet darkly excited depths of his as he stared down at her.

"Do you want me to leave you alone?"

His question was whispered against her lips as his mouth touched hers again and again—refusing to satisfy her by thoroughly claiming what she so readily offered. Why did he have to make her verbalize what was so evident by her actions? Her body arched against his convulsively as his hands trailed down her sides to rest on her firm buttocks, pressing her feverish body closer still to his own hard length, making her wholly aware of his need for her.

"Do you?" He persisted when she remained silent, running his tongue along the outline of her lips.

Aching pleasurably all over, she still held back admitting what he already knew. He sought her complete capitulation—mentally and physically—and she didn't have the strength to resist him.

"Why do you have to make me say it?" Her desire-laden voice was barely above a whisper.

"Because I need to hear it, and you need to admit it."

He took her lower lip between his teeth, pulling at her flesh slightly as his strong hands slowly slid up her body to rest at her waist. She moaned aloud, her fingers moving to the back of his head, pressing him closer.

As she pulled his lips to hers, she hissed into his mouth, "No—God help me—I don't want you to leave me alone."

At her admission, his smile deepened before her eyes closed and his lips claimed hers in a scorching kiss. She couldn't think or breathe—all she could do was feel. He sent the blood coursing through her veins boiling out of control with every touch. There wasn't a part of her that didn't belong to him and she was unashamedly glad about that.

She decided then and there to accept their mutual desire and try to make the best of their complicated relationship—while it lasted. She would focus on his being a man, her being a woman and on their sharing the basic needs, even though she reluctantly conceded that she wanted much more than that from him. But did he want more from her?

He rolled onto his back suddenly, taking her with him so that she was lying on top of him. His hands intertwined in her hair, withdrawing her clinging lips from his reluctantly. He smiled at her dazed, questioning expression.

"Touch me." At his soft command, he sensed rather than saw the rush of color that flooded her cheeks as she lowered her eyes demurely. "Alesha." His insistent calling of her name made her to look at him again. "Touch me."

As if spellbound by his tone and his request, she brought her hand up and ran her fingers lightly over his cheek. It was not long before she had memorized every curve, every line of his handsome face. She lowered her head and her lips and tongue slowly followed the path her fingers had left behind. She inhaled deeply at his neck, intoxicated by the clean smell of his flesh. She couldn't believe she was doing this—wanting and needing to do this. It was as if she were outside her body, watching someone else. She was unable to stop her investigation of his body, though, because what she was doing felt too good to end.

Her fingers lightly touched his chest before threading themselves in the short hair she found there, tugging lightly. His quick intake of breath told her she must be doing something right. She raked her long nails down the length of his chest before bringing them back up again. Then she lowered her head, tasting his salty flesh, slowly covering his chest and abdomen with wet kisses—thoroughly enjoying herself. Her tongue licked his lower stomach, sliding in and out of his belly button, but she was still too inhibited to explore any further, and though he longed for her to, he refrained from demanding more than she was able to give.

After several moments longer, she raised her head and lowered her lips toward his. As they touched, he started to take control of the kiss, but resisted the urge. He wanted her to realize she could arouse him and initiate intimacy instead of just responding to his advances. As her eyes stared deeply into his, her mouth continued its descent until their lips touched. Her hair fell over her face and his as she opened her mouth over his, kissing him amorously. His hands cupped her face, holding her closer as she continued to kiss him with mounting passion.

Her hands moved to cover his as they rested on her face, moving them to her breasts before moving her own to frame his face as they continued to kiss. He groaned at her initiative, his hands moving from her breasts to her hips, lifting her slightly before bringing her back down to engulf him totally.

She gasped and straightened to stare at him with passion-glazed eyes. His hands showed her how to please him and herself—for several long wonderful minutes she was in control of their passion and she reveled in it.

Suddenly, unable to bear her sweet torture another second, he reared up and rolled until she was beneath his hard, throbbing body and he took control of their passionate dance.

"You feel so good," he breathed into her mouth as his body bombarded hers.

She wanted to tell him he felt good, too, but coherent words eluded her. So, she just moaned in agreement. Incredible pleasure began to fill and overflow from her burning body once again. Trembling hands moved to his back, holding him tight. She pressed against him and draped one of her legs over his in order to bring him deeper into her as she pulsed around him, intensifying the pleasure with his every thrust. Nothing else mattered except the wonderful wildfire racing through her veins and the sound of Derrick's ragged, hoarse breath intermingling with hers. Nothing was important except the strong beating of his heart next to hers—nothing, except the rapture she experienced once again with him.

The next morning, she awakened with a heavy weight on her chest, which she soon realized was Derrick's head. One of his arms was draped casually across her waist, his eyes were closed and his breathing was even and steady, evidence that he was still asleep.

Her heart skipped several beats at the intimacy of their positions. She was tempted to awaken him, but stopped herself suddenly. Why would she choose a course of action she knew would lead to another passionate bout of lovemaking between them? As she gingerly smoothed a few tendrils of hair away from her eyes, she admitted that, even now, her body craved his. She should be exhausted, but she wasn't. She was becoming an addict, and his body was the drug she now needed more than anything else in the world. And, like all addicts, she didn't think she would be able to give him up until he nearly destroyed her.

Softly, her fingers moved to trace the outline of his sleeping face, remembering the sweet love they had made together last night. There had been a blending, a sharing of emotions that each of them was powerless to stop. Once she would have been troubled by that. Instead, the knowledge now made her happy and hopeful. Her heart somersaulted as she fought the impulse to slide down level with his face, kiss him awake and once again experience a bit of heaven in his arms.

She closed her eyes and sighed contentedly, enjoying the feel of him against her. She could lie here with him this close to her all day and never need to move. Her body had never felt so relaxed or so alive, nor had her soul. As her fingers lightly moved across his lips, she remembered the intense delight they had given her last night. She again fought against waking him so that she could experience the mind-boggling enjoyment she found only when they were pressed close as one. Despite her resolve not to, she silently admitted that she had lost a huge piece of her heart to him last night.

Quickly, she reopened her eyes, fingers stilling their exploration of his handsome outline. God, what was she doing? How had she allowed herself to reach this point? She hadn't meant to become emotionally involved with him again, and yet, against her better judgment, she had. It had been so easy and, what was more terrifying, she wasn't the least bit sorry that she had.

He was a good man and she was tired of fighting the fact that she needed and wanted him in her life. The real question was this: did he feel the same way about her? Once, she had been certain he had, but now, she didn't know how he felt about her. He wanted her, but what did he think about them being together permanently? She finally knew what she wanted without a doubt, but what did Derrick want?

Very slowly, she inched herself away from her husband's warm, inviting body. He stirred several times before rolling away from her onto his side of the bed. She waited a few moments and then carefully got up so as not to awaken him and donned a thin robe over her naked form. Immediately, she missed the heat of his body as the coldness of the room engulfed her.

Tiptoeing over to the thermostat, she adjusted it higher before walking quickly and quietly to the bathroom, softly closing the door behind her. Once there, she leaned against the door and let out a sigh, partly thankful that she had made it without waking him, and partly disappointed because she hadn't. She then flipped the light switch and was glad to see that the power had returned overnight.

Derrick lifted his head from the pillow and sat up in the bed. His fingers slowly retraced the spot on his face that Alesha had just caressed. He tamped down the urge to join her in the bathroom, realizing she needed some space and so did he.

Even as his body longed for hers, he resisted fulfilling the desire that was never far from his mind when he thought of his wife. Even though they had just been married a few days and had some important issues to resolve between them, she felt much more like his wife than the woman who had held the title before her. There were questions he still needed answers to—answers only she could give him—and he would get those answers soon. He had to, because his feelings for her were growing astronomically. He didn't know how to contain them. Did he even want to try?

* * *

An hour later, Alesha placed a glass of orange juice next to the plate of steaming pancakes she had just prepared for herself and Derrick. She shivered as she looked out at the snow-covered terrain beyond the window, and walked out of the kitchen to the foot of the stairs.

"Derrick, breakfast is ready," she yelled.

"I'll be right down."

She turned, went back into the kitchen and sat down. She had just taken a sip of her juice when he came through the door dressed casually in a Washington Redskins sweat suit. He stopped by her chair to kiss her cheek, nearly causing her to spill her juice before sitting down opposite her.

"Good morning." He smiled and looked out at the snowy day. "It's a good thing we don't have to go out today."

"Yes, it is." She watched him as he cut into a pancake and placed a large piece in his mouth—a mouth that had given her the most gratification she had ever known.

"Mmm, this is delicious," he said, breaking into her disturbing thoughts.

"Thank you."

There was welcome silence as he continued to eat and she pretended to do so. She felt so odd, as if they were really a married couple enjoying a leisurely breakfast together. Of course, they were, but this was hardly an ordinary relationship, she firmly reminded herself. However, she wished it was. Suddenly, she wanted to talk to him about little things, to have him smile at her without mockery, to freely touch him and to feel…

"Alesha?"

"I'm sorry, what?" She reluctantly roused herself from her disquieting contemplation.

He smiled then, that smile she hated—the one that said he knew exactly what she was thinking. Why did he seem to know her so well, at times even better than she knew herself?

"I said you're an excellent cook," he slowly reiterated, razor-sharp eyes studying her flushed features.

"Thanks." She smiled slightly, a little embarrassed.

"I missed you when I woke up."

His seemingly innocent sentence caught her off guard, making her drop her fork noisily onto the plate in front of her. She swallowed the lump in her throat and glanced up from her plate.

She stared into his eyes as warm color began to flood her cheeks and stammered, "I—I, um, well, you were out so late and I wanted to let you sleep in."

He smiled that shrewd smile before replying, "I know what you wanted."

Her pupils dilated to twice their normal size. Had he been awake when she had caressed his face? Had he known she had almost awakened him with kisses and an invitation not for food, but for herself? At that thought, her discomfiture increased almost unbearably.

"Would you like some more coffee?" She stood up, seeking an escape from his presence.

"Alesha, don't be afraid of me," he said, grabbing her hand as she prepared to walk past him, halting her progress.

"I'm not," she whispered without looking at him.

"Yes, you are," he softly contradicted, pulling on her hand until she was sitting in the chair next to his, forcing her to meet his intense gaze. "You're also afraid of yourself and of us," he correctly surmised.

"This is all so new to me." She didn't bother to deny his observation.

"It's new to me, too," he assured her.

"You were married before," she reminded him, daring to glance into his understanding face.

"Not like this," he said quickly, surprising himself and pleasing her.

"No?" Why did her heart skip a beat at his admission?

"No," he reiterated, refusing to elaborate. "It doesn't have to be an unpleasant experience."

"It's not," she replied before she could stop herself, waiting for a sarcastic response that never came. Instead, he smiled at her more gently than he ever had. In doing so, he melted her heart.

"And that's what bothers you."

"Yes," she replied truthfully, unable to look away from his irresistible eyes.

His free hand moved to lightly touch her warm cheek as he suggested, "Stop berating yourself for what you feel as far as we're concerned."

"I don't know if I can."

She couldn't believe they were having a serious soul-searching conversation. It was a novel, yet welcome, experience.

"Maybe it will help if you know that I feel the same way, too," he admitted.

"Do you?" Surprised eyes stared deeply into his warm ones.

"Yes, I do." He brought her hand to his lips. "We both know why we married, but what we have together is real—as real as it can get. There's no shame in admitting that."

He was being so kind to her—she didn't know what to say. This was the last thing she had expected when she had bared her soul. It added just one more layer of confusion to her already troubled heart.

"It feels real." She sighed softly.

"It is real." He traced the outline of her lower lip with his fingers. "We're the only two people who will ever know what we feel when we're together. I promise I won't ever use that knowledge against you, or make you sorry for wanting me."

"You're shattering all my evil illusions about you, Derrick Chandler." Her voice was husky with emotion as she fought back tears his compassionate words evoked.

"Good. You should have none when it comes to people. You should make up your own mind."

The smile he gave her was tender and, dare she think it, loving. She felt her heart melt even further at the look he gave her, and knew she was very rapidly losing her battle not to become any more emotionally involved with him.

"You're right."

"Let's take it one day at a time," he suggested.

He continued to smile, not the smile she hated, but one she knew she could definitely learn to love.

"One day at a time." She raised her glass of juice and lightly touched it with his before taking a sip.

Their eyes locked and held. She felt raw and wonderfully alive. She suddenly knew she was fighting a losing battle as far as he was concerned. In such a short time, he had completely insinuated himself into her life and, more importantly, her heart. She doubted she would ever be able to totally extricate herself again and wondered if she even wanted to try.

Chapter 10

They had returned from Derrick's country house a month ago and their life had switched into high gear. Their days were full with campaigning, and their nights were full of unbelievable passion. Derrick smiled as he contemplated being alone with his wife tonight. Thoughts of her caused the days to linger interminably and being with her made the nights go by much too quickly.

His smile was replaced by a frown as he riffled through a ton of mail that had accumulated since yesterday. He was grateful to be interrupted by the buzz of the intercom.

"Yes, Dorothy, what is it?"

"Sir, Mrs. Chandler is here."

He frowned at his assistant's strange tone. "Send her in."

"Yes, sir."

He stood and walked from behind his desk. When the door opened, the smile that had been plastered on his face changed into a shocked frown as a tall, slender woman sauntered into his office.

"Hello, Derrick."

"Diana. This is a…"

She smiled brightly. "Pleasure?"

"Surprise."

She kissed his stiff cheek. "A good one, I hope."

He reclined against his desk. "What are you doing here?"

"You know I've been out of the country."

"No—" he shook his head "—I didn't."

"I just got back to the States and imagine my surprise when I saw my husband's picture plastered all over the news."

He raised an eyebrow. "Ex-husband."

"Anyway—" she walked closer "—I just had to see you."

"Why?"

"To congratulate you on your senatorial run. The polls say your chances are excellent."

"A phone call would have sufficed."

"I know." She placed a hand on his thigh. "But I like the personal touch."

"What's with calling yourself Mrs. Chandler?" He pointedly removed her hand. "You didn't use my name when we were together."

"I wanted to make sure you would see me."

"I would have seen you."

She smiled. "That's good to know."

"There's something else you should know."

She leaned toward him. "What?"

"There is a new Mrs. Chandler in my life."

"Yes." She ran fingers through her short hair. "I've heard you remarried."

"I did." He stood, walked around his desk and sat down.

"So, how's married life treating you the second time around?"

"Great."

"Really?" She sat on the edge of his desk and crossed her long legs.

He smiled. "Really."

"I can't wait to meet her."

"Why?"

She shrugged. "I'm just curious."

"Don't be." He picked up an envelope from his desk. "If you'll excuse me, I have a lot of work to do."

"I thought we could catch up."

He shook his head. "We don't have anything to catch up on."

She smiled at his bent head and stood. "All right. I'll be seeing you around, Derrick."

"I doubt it." He glanced at her briefly. "We run in different circles."

"You never know." She blew him a kiss and left.

Once he was alone, he slammed the folder shut and glared at the closed door. This unexpected, unpleasant turn of events was the last thing he needed.

"Damn!"

Alesha took a glass of champagne from a passing waiter. She made her way onto the covered and heated balcony while Derrick and Cam talked with a donor inside the ballroom. Tonight, they were attending another in a long line of political fundraisers.

"Hello, Alesha."

She turned and smiled at the woman who touched her arm. She was tall with short hair and smooth brown skin, and she wore a red figure-hugging, low-cut sequined gown that made Alesha's long-sleeved black dress seem dowdy by comparison.

"Hello, do I know you?"

"We haven't been formally introduced." The woman smiled. "Nice party, isn't it?"

Alesha returned her smile. "Very."

"I prefer quieter, more intimate settings, myself."

"So do I, but this is the political life," Alesha said, laughing. "Are you here alone?"

"Mmm." She sipped her drink. "Yes, I wanted to hear Derrick speak in person."

Alesha's eyebrow rose at the woman's familiar use of her husband's name. "Do you know Derrick?"

"You could say that," the woman said, smiling secretively. "I'm sorry. Allow me to introduce myself." She paused for maximal effect before revealing, "I'm Diana Chandler."

Alesha choked on her drink. "Who?"

"Diana Chandler." She smiled at her discomfiture. "I guess I should say Diana Davis-Chandler."

Her eyes widened. "You're Derrick's ex-wife?"

"Yes. I'm sorry if I shocked you."

Alesha knew she wasn't sorry at all. Diana had deliberately sought her out to announce herself. The question was, why hadn't Derrick told her?

"Didn't Derrick tell you I was back in town?"

"No." Alesha shook her head. "No, he didn't."

"Well—" she shrugged dismissively "—I'm sure it just slipped his mind."

"It must have."

She placed a hand on her hip. "So you're the new Mrs."

"Yes, I am."

"We must trade stories some time."

"I don't think so." Alesha placed her half-empty glass on a passing waiter's tray. "Excuse me."

"Surely. It was nice to meet you."

She didn't return Diana's sentiments as she walked away quickly. Why hadn't Derrick told her his ex was in town?

Had he been meeting secretly with her? What did she want? As she reentered the ballroom, her arm was grabbed by a familiar hand.

"Alesha, where have you been?"

"On the patio."

Derrick glanced at her distraught face. "What's wrong?"

"Nothing." She shook her head.

"Come on, Alesha. What is it?"

"I just met Diana."

He frowned. "She's here?"

"Yes." She stared at him. "Why didn't you tell me she was in town?"

"There was no reason to."

She glared at him. "No reason to?"

"No." He studied her closely. "What did she say to you?"

"Nothing."

"Alesha…"

"I need to get out of here, Derrick. Now!" She pulled her arm free and ran from the room.

Diana watched the scene from across the room gleefully. Derrick encountered her smiling eyes and shot her an angry glare before following his wife out.

They entered their house and Alesha angrily threw her purse and coat down on the hall table before stalking into the living room. Derrick sighed and followed her slowly.

"How long am I going to get the silent treatment?"

She turned from the window to glare at him. "You want to talk?" At his positive nod, she obliged him. "Fine! Why didn't you tell me Diana was in town?"

He sighed. "Her comings and goings don't have anything to do with me or, more importantly, us."

"Derrick." She walked closer. "I deserved to know!"

"Why?"

"Why?" She spread her hands wide. "Oh, I don't know. Maybe so I would be prepared for a woman accosting me at a fundraiser claiming to be Mrs. Chandler!"

He scowled. "She didn't."

"She did!"

Anger darkened his eyes. "Damn that woman!"

"Damn you both!"

"Alesha." He deliberately kept his voice measured. "I didn't know she was going to be there tonight."

"But you knew she was in town!"

"I only found out today."

"That was long enough to tell me, Derrick!"

"Dammit, I didn't see a reason to tell you!" His frustration was evident. "As far as I was concerned, I didn't expect to see her again."

She eyed him suspiciously. "Of course you didn't."

He frowned. "What is that supposed to mean?"

"I'm sure you can figure it out."

"Will you stop behaving so irrationally?"

"I'm sorry that I'm not cold and sophisticated enough for you."

"What are you talking about? I didn't say that."

"You implied it." She was angry and hurt, and she didn't want to be reasonable. "If my company displeases you so much, why don't you go and find Diana? I'm sure she'll accommodate you any way she can."

She pushed past him, but he grabbed her arm, halting her retreat. Her eyes sparkled furiously.

"Don't be an idiot!" he said.

She gasped. "So now I'm an idiot?"

She tried to pull her arm free. He refused to release her, pulling her closer instead.

"You are if you think I want anything to do with Diana."

"You married her."

He had married Diana voluntarily—it hadn't been an antiseptic arrangement, like their marriage.

"I also divorced her—quickly."

"Do you regret that decision?"

Damn, he thought they were beyond nonsense like this. He had hoped they were building something special and permanent over the past months. They had been before Diana's sudden reappearance in his life.

She held her breath and waited for his response. A response she dreaded yet needed to hear. His prolonged silence sent fingers of fear dancing up her spine.

"Where are these absurd questions coming from?"

"Answer me!"

He squared his shoulders. "No, I don't think I will."

They stubbornly stared at each other for a few pregnant seconds before she pulled her arm from his and stalked from the room. He followed.

"Where are you going?"

"To bed." She paused before pointedly adding, "Alone!"

"Alesha…"

"I don't want to talk to you anymore tonight!"

"That's fine with me!" He grabbed his keys from the table.

She paused on the stairs. "Where are you going?"

"Do you care?"

"No, I don't care at all." She continued up the stairs.

"Good!" He stormed out, slamming the door behind him.

Early the next morning, Alesha was sitting on the sofa in her robe, drinking her second cup of coffee when she heard the front door open. Seconds later, Derrick walked into the room, disheveled, still dressed in his tuxedo from the night before. He looked exhausted. He barely glanced at her as he walked over and poured himself a cup of black coffee.

"Where were you last night?"

"Why?" His voice was terse.

Her lips thinned. "Were you with her?"

He made contact eye contact with her. "With whom?"

"With Diana."

"You sound like you're jealous." He watched her closely. "But that's impossible, isn't it?"

She lowered her eyes. "Of course it is."

"Yeah, it would be since our marriage isn't real, is it?"

His observation cut her to the quick. To her, their marriage was very real—she had thought he felt the same way. With superhuman effort, she turned to him with a frosty expression.

"You know the answer to that."

His eyes burned. "We're just playing house, aren't we?"

"Yes." She picked up her juice and resisted an urge to throw it in his face.

"Then why do you care where I was?" He nearly shouted the question, angered by her response.

"I don't." She smiled coldly. "You can stay with Diana, for all I care."

"I wasn't with Diana!" He slammed his cup down hard, sloshing liquid onto the table.

"Is that right?"

"Yes, that's right!" At her disbelieving stare he swore savagely, "Dammit, nothing is going on between us and if you don't believe me, then that's your problem!"

Before she could respond, she watched Derrick turn and angrily walk up the stairs, two at a time. Was he telling the truth? She wanted to believe him with every breath she took, but could she trust him? She had before Diana's arrival. Should she now?

* * *

Cam watched as Derrick continued pacing angrily in front of his desk.

"What's the matter with you?"

"Nothing!"

"Really?" An eyebrow rose in disbelief. "Is that why you look like you're contemplating murder?"

"Maybe I am."

"Who's the target?"

Derrick leaned against his desk. "Diana."

Cam frowned. "Diana who?"

"Davis."

"What?" Cam stood to face his angry friend. "Is she in town?"

"Unfortunately."

"What has she done?"

"She was at the fundraiser last night and accosted Alesha."

"Oh, no." Cam rolled his eyes. "Tell me all about it."

"She introduced herself to Alesha as Mrs. Chandler!"

"That woman!" Cam shook his head in exasperation.

"Alesha and I had a fight last night. She's angry because I didn't tell her Diana was in town."

"When did you find out?"

"Yesterday afternoon. She came by my office."

"Why didn't you tell Alesha?"

"I had hoped she would just go away."

Cam sighed. "Wishful thinking."

"I should find her and wring her neck!"

"No." Cam placed a hand on Derrick's shoulder. "Just stay away from her. She's nothing but trouble."

He sighed. "You're right."

"Nice to hear you admit it for once."

Derrick continued to frown. His friend's attempt at humor was completely lost on him.

"What does she want, Cam?"

He shrugged. "Running for office is just like winning the lottery—people come out from the woodwork, trying to latch onto your coattails."

"I suppose, but she's not going to ruin my marriage."

"Your marriage of convenience?"

Derrick silently cursed his slip of the tongue. He had enough trouble right now without getting into a philosophical discussion with his friend about the status of his marriage.

"I'm not going to let her screw up my election chances."

Cam smiled. "No, you had it right the first time."

"Cameron…"

He laughed. "Save your protestations for someone else."

Derrick rubbed his tired eyes. "How did everything get so out of control?"

"It's called life, my friend." He patted Derrick's shoulder comfortingly.

Derrick reopened determined eyes. "I'm not going to let Diana demolish what I've worked so hard to build."

"I hope not." He couldn't resist adding, "What you and Alesha have is special, but then, I don't have to tell you that, do I?"

Derrick sighed heavily. "This has nothing to do with Alesha."

"Oh, man, why don't you stop lying to yourself?" Cam shook his head in remonstration. "You care about your wife very much and if you won't admit it to me, at least admit it to yourself."

Derrick made eye contact with his friend, but remained silent. There was no need to say a word because they both knew he was right. The question was, what was he going to do about it?

That afternoon Alesha smiled wistfully as she listened to the antics of her onetime colleague, related as only Angela could. She hadn't seen Angela since the wedding and had missed her terribly, but she wasn't miserable in her new life as she had thought she would be—that is, not until Diana had shown up.

"So, how's married life?"

"Great." She forced a smile.

"I should be so lucky to find a guy like Derrick." Angela took a sip of her water.

"There are other fish in the ocean. What about Cam?"

"Derrick's friend?"

"Yes, the man who took great care placing my garter on your thigh at my wedding."

"Oh, yeah. I remember him." Angela smiled secretively. "He's very cute."

"I noticed."

"Really? What else did you notice?" Alesha leaned forward.

"Nothing."

"So did you two talk?"

"We exchanged a few words."

"And?"

"And nothing. You've already taken the top prize."

"And I intend to keep him." Her teasing smile faltered slightly when she realized how much she meant the words she had so easily spoken.

"I didn't doubt that for a moment." Angela's smile turned to a frown. "Hey, what's wrong?"

Alesha blinked rapidly. She had been trying with all her might to appear carefree and happy, and had thought she was doing an admirable job until Angela's question.

"Nothing's wrong." She sipped her drink. "Why would you think that?"

"Something's bothering you." She frowned. "What is it?"

"It's…"

"Don't you dare say 'nothing'!" Angela touched her hand. "Tell me."

She remained silent as she contemplated answering her friend's question. The truth was, she needed to talk to someone and Angela was her confidante. She would keep her secret. Besides, she could use some wise advice right about now.

"Derrick and I went to a fundraiser last night."

"And?"

"His ex-wife was there."

Angela's mouth dropped open in shock. "He was married before?"

"Briefly, two years ago."

"Did you know?"

"Of course," she said.

Angela frowned suspiciously. "What did she do to you?"

She sighed. "She introduced herself as Diana Chandler."

Angela gawked. "No, that hussy didn't!"

Alesha chuckled at her choice of words. "She did."

"The nerve of her!"

Alesha sipped her drink. "Oh, she has plenty of that."

"What did Derrick do?"

"He wasn't around when we met."

"Well, you don't have anything to worry about."

"I don't?"

"Of course not. Anyone seeing you and Derrick together can see you're meant to be."

"We are?"

"Definitely. His ex is just jealous that you have what she couldn't hold on to."

"I suppose you're right." Alesha prayed she was right.

"You're not worried about her, are you?"

"No."

"No?"

She sighed. "Maybe a little bit."

"Did you talk to Derrick?" After Alesha nodded, Angela said, "What did he say?"

She left out all the colorful language and shouting and succinctly responded, "That he's not interested in her."

"Of course he's not. I rest my case." She frowned at her friend. "You do believe him, don't you?"

"Of course. It was just unnerving meeting her out of the blue."

"I'm sure it was, but, girl, Derrick is so hung up on you he's not going to let anyone come between you, especially not his ex-wife." She paused. "And *ex* is the operative word."

"I know." She smiled. "You're right."

"Of course I'm right. Diana is just trying to stir up trouble where none exists. Don't give her the satisfaction. You're Mrs. Chandler now—not her."

"Yes, I am," she said, smilingly.

"And don't you forget it," Angela ordered.

"I won't," Alesha promised, and that was one promise she intended to keep.

Alesha returned home a little after 7:00 p.m. after making several appearances at different functions and giving a speech at a women's club—all after her much-needed lunch with Angela. She was exhausted.

She kicked off her black high-heel pumps and walked into the living room. There, she threw her purse and keys onto the tabletop and limply fell onto the plush black-leather sofa, closing her eyes contentedly as she let out her breath on a deep, grateful sigh. Thankfully, Derrick wasn't home—she didn't have the strength to fight with him again.

They needed to talk about Diana, but she promised herself that when they did, they would do it civilly. She grimaced at the thought of the woman who had upset the tenuous balance of their world. What did Diana want? She silently reprimanded herself. It was obvious that she wanted Derrick. The question was, did he want her? A queasy feeling invaded her stomach as she considered the last question. He said he didn't. He gave no indication that he did. She wanted to believe him, but should she?

"Rough day?"

She opened her eyes to stare into Derrick's, not realizing she had briefly dozed off. He was smiling down at her with a bouquet of red roses and thankfully appeared to be in a better mood than he had been that morning. Frankly, so was she after her lunch with Angela. Maybe Cam had calmed him down. She hoped so.

She sat up and tucked her legs beneath her. "Are those for me?"

"Yes." He handed her the flowers. "They're a peace offering.

"Thank you." She smiled. "Derrick, about last night and this morning…"

"Alesha." He sat down on the coffee table in front of her. "I don't want to argue with you again."

"Neither do I." She sighed in relief. "I'm sorry."

"Me, too." He paused before admitting, "I should have told you about Diana."

She watched him closely. "Why didn't you?"

"I honestly didn't think I would see her again, or that you two would ever meet."

"Why is she here, Derrick?"

"I don't know and I don't care, but it has nothing to do with me or us."

She fingered a soft petal. "Doesn't it?"

"Not as far as I'm concerned." He touched her hand and serious eyes bore into hers. "I'm not interested in Diana. Do you believe me?"

She nodded slowly. "Yes, I do."

He smiled in relief. "Good." He kissed her briefly before standing and going to the bar.

"Does it really matter to you what I think?"

"Yes, it does." He turned to stare at her. "For the record, I spent the night in my car, which is why I was in such a foul mood this morning."

His words were like music to her ears. She had suffered last night and today, envisioning him with that witch, Diana.

"Why did you do that?"

He smiled sheepishly. "To teach you a lesson."

She laughed. "I think I got the better end of the stick—I slept in our nice, comfy bed."

His eyes darkened. "I'll join you tonight."

She blushed before changing the subject. "Um, I saw Angela today."

"How is she?" He noisily dropped a few pieces of ice in a glass.

"She's Angela." She chuckled and he joined her.

"Can I get you something?"

"No, thanks." All she wanted to do was to stay where she was and continue their polite conversation.

"We'll have to invite her to dinner soon."

"That would be nice. Maybe we can invite Cam, too."

"Matchmaking?" He sipped his drink and walked back toward her. A whimsical smile tilted the corners of his mouth.

"No, not really."

"No?"

"Well, maybe a little," she confessed.

He sat down beside her on the sofa, placed his drink on the side table and pulled her legs across his lap, forcing her to lean back, and softly began massaging her weary feet and legs. She started to protest, but what he was doing felt so wonderful. She sank into the cushions and watched him through half-closed eyes.

"Oh!" She moaned gratefully, instantly forgetting what they had been talking about. "That feels wonderful."

He smiled at her and continued in silence. His strong fingers kneaded her tired flesh until it was putty in his hands. His fingers slid up and down the soles of her aching feet before moving to her ankles, making soothing little circles on her silky skin.

"How was your day?" She fully opened her eyes to stare at his handsome profile.

"Very profitable."

He glanced at her shortly before returning his eyes to her legs. His magical fingers continued massaging her calves.

"Perhaps you're in the wrong line of business." She sighed dreamily.

He frowned at that and turned to stare at her. "Why do you say that?"

"You should be a masseur."

He laughed out loud, a pleasing sound she never tired of hearing. "You think so?" He ran his hands forcefully up and down her tingling calves.

"Oh, yes." She nearly purred the words.

His hands moved up to her thighs underneath the wool skirt she wore, suddenly causing a different kind of sensation—a familiar pain began growing in the pit of her stomach. His warm, strong hands caressed her inner thighs.

She stared longingly into the darkening intensity of his eyes and knew he was thinking the same thing she was. She realized how this encounter was going to end, and she welcomed it. She silently admitted she had been secretly waiting for this moment all day long.

Suddenly, there was a knock at the door followed by the entrance of their housekeeper. "Excuse me, sir, ma'am.

There's a call for you, Mr. Chandler." She handed Derrick the phone before soundlessly leaving.

Derrick absently continued to rub her legs, and she watched him unobtrusively. She bet he could charm a snake out of its skin without even trying. She half listened to his conversation and realized that he was talking to Cam. She prayed they would not have to go out for the evening—she just didn't have the strength.

"Yes, Cam, everything is fine." He smiled at her. "Thanks, but we're looking forward to an evening alone."

She could have kissed him for refusing Cam's invitation.

"Alesha's had a rough day and I'm tired, too," he explained and then drily laughed. "Yes, Cameron."

He hung up and stared at her. His hands reached out and grabbed hers, pulling her until she was sitting upright. Her legs were still draped over his thighs. Her face was inches away from his. They stared at each other intensely. Whenever he was near, she completely forgot everything, except for the wonderful way he made her feel. She held her breath, waiting and longing for him to kiss her. Just the slightest movement on her part and their lips would touch. However, neither of them moved to initiate it.

"Cam says hello." He traced her cheek with his thumb, setting off little eruptions within her.

"Oh."

"Hmm." His fingers moved to her burgundy lips, taking extreme care to outline every curve. "What do you want to do tonight?"

"Let's stay in."

"And do what?"

Enigmatic eyes stared into her aroused ones. His voice was low and sexy. It touched her in all the right places.

"Let's make some popcorn and watch a good movie," she said.

He smiled. "That sounds like a good start."

"Yes."

He stood, took her hand and pulled her up with him. "But after the movie, I get to decide what we do next."

Her pupils dilated and she leaned toward him. "Deal."

They smiled at each other, both glad the unpleasantness of last night was behind them. He placed a quick kiss on her lips before leading her out into the hallway.

Chapter 11

They sat side by side on a soft black-leather sofa, watching a horror movie. The lights were off and the atmosphere in the room was both eerie and romantic. At a particularly scary part, Alesha screamed and automatically sought out the comfort of Derrick's chest, hiding her face there. He laughed at her, but his arm went around her shoulders as he pulled her closer.

"It's all right."

She felt him smile against her hair. Suddenly realizing the intimacy of their positions, she prepared to move away. His arm, however, tightened around her shoulders, pulling her closer.

"Don't move."

She didn't want to move from his comforting presence. So she did as he indicated and stayed right where she was. Tucking her legs underneath her, she turned her head until her cheek was resting on his warm chest and she continued to watch the movie.

She felt and heard the strong thudding of his heart. That wonderfully woodsy-smelling cologne he wore drifted up to tickle her nose, almost tempting her to unbutton his shirt and bury her face in his muscular chest until she was absorbed by his intoxicating smell.

His hand absently massaged her shoulder before moving to lightly play with her hair. Early in their relationship, she had realized that he liked to do that, just as much as she liked for him to. She inhaled deeply, again assaulting her senses with his scent. Suddenly, even though she was enjoying the film, the last thing she wanted was to finish watching it. Before she gave in to an irrepressible urge to pull his mouth down to hers, she abruptly stood, taking them both by surprise.

"I'm going to get some more tea." She answered his questioning gaze.

He grabbed her hand as he, too, stood. He noted the slight flush to her face and the pulse beating erratically at her neck. He longed to place his lips on that spot. He instinctively knew that she wanted him to do that, too—that and much more.

"No, you don't want any tea." His arms pulled her close.

His lips found and enclosed hers. She didn't even pretend to resist, sighing in pleasure against his mouth. Her hands drifted upward to rest on his chest. She felt herself sinking to the floor and her hands trailed up to his sturdy shoulders as they continued to engage in a thoroughly enjoyable embrace.

Against her will, he removed his lips from hers and firmly responded, "You want this—you want me."

She was unable to respond as his sizzling mouth covered hers again. He had to be the most fabulous kisser in the world, she thought. She felt herself leaving her body. His touch inflamed her soul, making her feel as if she were the most important person in his life. As her arms encircled his neck, she silently prayed that assumption was correct. Her eyes closed against the blazing heat emanating from his gaze.

"Yes, I do want you," she unashamedly admitted. "I want you very much."

They both lay close together on the softly carpeted floor. His lips fused against hers, their tongues engaged in a heated dance of rising passion. Her mouth caressed his. Once again she felt consumed by him and longed to feel only as he could make her feel. They savored the tastes and textures of each other's mouths.

His hands moved down her back to her softly rounded bottom, to the back of her thigh, intimately draping one of her legs over his, pressing her firmly against his solid length, making her fully aware of the hardening bulge in his groin. His body telegraphed a wild need for hers, a need that matched hers for him.

His roving hands moved to unbutton the front of her blouse with expert ease, slipping beneath to explore her breasts. His lips placed tender kisses down her cheek to her neck before his teeth bit into a pebble-hard nipple through the sheer lacy fabric of her bra. She closed her eyes tighter as mounting pleasure built unbearably within her tingling body.

Her fingers flexed on his shoulders before moving under his T-shirt to caress his chest before exploring his muscular back, her nails raking across his taut skin as her hunger for him surged. His hot mouth teased her flesh until she thought she would explode.

She moaned aloud, clinging to him, begging him with her body to make love to her. In response, his mouth blazed a trail of fire up her trembling body to capture her lips once again, plundering her. One of his legs eased intimately between hers and he rolled until he was half lying on top of her, crushing her body into the floor as he ravaged her mouth. She wanted him so much that it physically hurt and it was a heady feeling knowing that he wanted her just as much.

Her body molded against his perfectly. She clung to him, moaning. His caresses grew more ardent, more insistent. His hands slid down to her hips and then moved to the front of her jeans, slipping under the waistband to stroke the smooth flesh he found there.

His mouth bruised hers, but she didn't care. All she wanted was him—always him and only him. She sighed as her naked chest and abdomen moved against his. She longed to feel his naked body imprinting itself on hers. Her hands moved to his firm bottom, pressing closer to his rock-hard length, silently pleading with him to give them both what they so desperately wanted and needed.

She felt him smile slightly at her actions and she didn't care if he knew how much she wanted him. Nothing mattered except the completeness she felt every time his body claimed hers.

Neither of them heard the doorbell ring, or the door open and close, because they were so engrossed with each other. Neither of them saw the man who entered and stood staring down at them in total shock. Neither of them heard his swiftly indrawn breath. Not until he spoke did they realize they were no longer alone.

"Excuse me!"

Simultaneously they turned passion-glazed eyes to stare reluctantly at Robert. He glanced away, but not until he encountered their intimately entwined limbs and his sister's unbuttoned blouse. Her arms were holding the man who had blackmailed her into marriage and his were around her.

It was Derrick who spoke first, the expression on his face

turning from passionate to annoyed, and then to amused. He sat up and faced Alesha's brother. This was going to be interesting.

"Robert, what are you doing here?" He almost laughed at the look of distaste on the other man's face.

Alesha was mortified! She sat up and shakily rebuttoned her blouse, grateful that Derrick was sitting in front of her, shielding her from her brother's gaze. Her head was lowered and she smoothed her hair, which had seconds before been disarrayed by Derrick's fingers. She couldn't bring herself to look at either man. Derrick grasped her hands once she had finished buttoning her blouse, and they both stood to face her brother.

"What's going on here?"

"What does it look like?" Derrick's disdain was evident. "I was about to make love to my wife," he told Robert.

Robert's eyes darkened in fury and he lunged for Derrick, snarling, "Why you son of a…"

Alesha quickly positioned her small frame between them and exclaimed with her back to Derrick, "Stop it!"

Derrick's hands automatically moved to her waist, encircling it, making Robert aware that she was his wife—a wife whom he could touch anytime he pleased.

Alesha didn't move away, seeking to forestall any further scene between them. Instead, she asked her brother, "Robert, why are you here?"

"To see how you're doing." His eyes narrowed as they darted to Derrick's hands still encircling her waist, his flat palm resting on her stomach possessively.

"As you can see, we were doing fine before we were interrupted." Derrick's hand possessively pulled her back against him.

"Derrick, please." She turned to stare at him. "Let me speak with Robert alone."

"You don't have to ask his permission!"

"Nor does she have to explain anything to you." Derrick smiled at Robert's indignation. "Whatever predicament Alesha finds herself in is not her fault—it's yours."

"Why, you..." Robert began moving toward Derrick again.

"Derrick, Robert, stop it!" Alesha placed a hand on each one's chest, trying to keep them apart.

"Alesha, I need to speak with you—alone," Robert said pointedly, his eyes spitting darts at her husband, who smiled at his expression, infuriating the other man more.

"Derrick, please leave us alone." She turned to look at him imploringly, both of her hands now on his chest.

He looked as if he were about to refuse, but something in her eyes made him relent. She could automatically sense this. It was remarkable how she had learned to read him—when he wanted her to, she amended. She lowered her hands from his chest, knowing he was about to acquiesce to her request.

"I'll be upstairs in *our bedroom*." Then, for Robert's benefit and his own pleasure, he bent and kissed her on the mouth before leaving.

Without preamble, Robert began, "What on earth are you doing?"

"What do you mean?"

"You're sleeping with him!"

She defiantly shot back, "Of course I am—I'm his wife. What did you expect?"

"I thought he would have some scruples!" Robert didn't bother to lower his voice.

"Oh, Robert, for heaven's sake!" She raked shaky fingers through her mussed hair. "Derrick's running for office. He can't be seen around town with other women when he's married to me. So I have to perform my wifely duties." She resented having to explain her relationship with her husband to him.

"I can't believe what I'm hearing! You're defending him? What happened to my little sister?"

"She grew up."

"How can you allow him to touch you?" Robert refused to comprehend her behavior.

One word quickly sprang to her mind to answer her brother's question—*easily*. It was no hardship experiencing Derrick's touch, just as it wasn't repugnant living with him as his wife and his lover.

"How could I stop him?" She wished he would leave.

"Do you mean he forces himself..."

"No." She shook her head.

"Then what?" He motioned with his hands, begging for understanding.

She closed her eyes and then opened them again to stare at her brother. "Robert, I'm his wife." She prayed he would leave it at that. He didn't.

"So? You're not his possession." He grabbed her shoulders and shook her slightly.

She pulled out of his grasp. "What do you want from me?"

"I want you to come with me. We have to get you out of here." He grabbed her hand.

"No!"

She wrenched her hand from him. His suggestion was repulsive to her. She didn't stop to consider why.

"Why not?"

"Have you forgotten why I married him?"

"It doesn't matter any longer."

"It does matter!" she responded hotly. "I won't have Mom find out what either of us has done. It would kill her."

"Sis, you've got to listen..."

"No, you listen." Her voice was deadly serious, though quiet. "I am not going to leave Derrick."

"Why not?"

She evaded his eyes. "Because I'm not."

"That's not an answer, Alesha." He watched her closely and illumination widened his eyes. "Do you want to stay here? Is that it?"

That was exactly it, but how could she admit that to him? Would he understand that the man she had married to cover up her brother's theft was a man she never wanted to be parted from?

"Robert, I'm not going to discuss my marriage with you."

"Alesha…"

"Robert, I love you." Her voice lost much of its sting. "But I don't want to hear another word from you about this—okay?" At his reluctant nod, she kissed his cheek. "Good. I'll talk to you later."

She turned and walked up the stairs, leaving him staring after her. He wouldn't have believed it had he not witnessed it—she cared for Derrick and, from the scene he had interrupted, Derrick felt something for her, too. He smiled slightly before walking to the front door. Damned if he had expected this turn of events. And he doubted that either of them had.

As she slowly entered the bedroom, she found Derrick sitting on the sofa by the window, papers strewn around him. He looked up.

"How did it go?" He walked over to her.

"All right." She walked away from him to sit at her vanity table.

He frowned. "Just all right?"

"Do you want a blow by blow?" She didn't want to talk about Robert. She needed to think.

"I want to know if I should expect another visit from your brother."

"Don't worry. I don't think Robert will be back without an invitation."

"Good." His response was brief and cool.

He watched her. As usual, when he was around his wife, strange emotions began to surface in him. Why did he have an almost overwhelming urge to simply hold her and tell her everything would be all right?

Without thinking, he reached out and placed a hand lightly on her shoulder. She jumped from the unexpected contact and he immediately removed his fingers, the kind words he had been about to utter vanishing just as suddenly as they had appeared.

"Don't worry. I'm not going to try to finish what we started downstairs."

He turned and walked toward the door, stopping to pick up his papers from the sofa. He was obviously angry. She glanced up and encountered his cool eyes in the mirror.

"Where are you going?"

"To the study to finish my speech for tomorrow night." He turned away. Something made him turn and face her again. "Unless you want me to stay."

She hesitated shortly before responding. What she really wanted was for him to hold her close and make her forget everything except him. However, she couldn't admit that. Or, more to the point, she wouldn't.

"You go ahead. I think I'll turn in." She lowered her eyes so that he wouldn't glimpse the misery behind them.

"Good night, then."

When she raised her eyes again, he was gone. She lowered her aching head into her hand, trying to make sense out of the situation. Her feelings were so jumbled, so mixed-up. If anyone asked her what day it was, she didn't think she would be able to correctly tell them. Just when she had come to some sort of inner peace about her relationship with Derrick, it seemed that life was throwing up obstacle after obstacle to undermine her tenuous hold on happiness.

She slowly stood and walked over to the bed before sitting down heavily on it. She stared at the door through which Derrick had exited moments earlier. She wanted to ask him what she meant to him. Where did he see their marriage going, if anywhere? Was she more to him than just a means to get elected? She wanted to ask all those things, but she couldn't—not until she was ready to impart a few truths of her own. She wanted to bare her soul to him, but she was afraid of being rejected. She knew he desired her, but did his feelings go any deeper than that?

Things had been going so well on their honeymoon, but ever since they had returned, the fragile happiness and peace they had attained had been sorely tested by outside forces, namely Diana and now Robert. Her feelings for Derrick placed her in enough inner turmoil—she didn't need anything or anyone adding to her already confused state.

One monumental certainty pierced through the fog of her mind—she wanted to remain Mrs. Chandler. Derrick wanted her physically, but did he want a life with her forever? The answer to that single question held the key to her future happiness.

Derrick stared blankly at the pages in front of him. His mind continued to stray to Alesha. Her demeanor a short while ago had baffled and angered him. She was so damn frustrating! Didn't she realize how much he wanted her?

"Dammit!" He hit the top of his desk in frustration. Last night it had been Diana and tonight Robert who had caused unnecessary friction between him and his wife. He seriously entertained the thought of whisking her away from everything and everyone. They seemed to get along so much better when they were all alone. Since they had returned to civilization, all they seemed to do was fight, and he hated that.

At that thought, he tried reminding himself that he was using Alesha as a means to an end—that was all. But he knew he was lying. He could no more stop caring about her than he could stop breathing. He had thought of little else for the years they had been separated. Now that they were together again, she had easily and quickly become an essential part of his life.

He looked forward to coming home to her and talking with her. He loved the fresh way she made everything seem to him. Most of all, he delighted in the way she made him feel. When they made love, there was an undeniable blending of hearts and minds. When they touched on purpose or accidentally, something dormant in him sprang to life—instinctively, he knew it was the same way for her. He needed her. She was crucial to his well-being and his happiness.

God, when had he lost control? What was he going to do to get it back? He sighed as he admitted he had never had any control as far as Alesha was concerned. There was no use in lying to himself anymore about that.

He glanced at his watch and his eyes wandered to the papers strewn carelessly on his desk. He hadn't gotten a thing done. All he had accomplished in the past two and a half hours was to think about Alesha. Sighing once again, he stood and rubbed his tired eyes. All he wanted to do was go to bed, lie down next to his wife and feel complete and whole as only she could make him feel.

She heard the bedroom door opening as Derrick came in. She was lying in bed on her back, pretending to be asleep. She heard him stop beside her before going into the bathroom, closing the door behind him. Seconds later, she heard the shower running.

She lay there, wanting to tell him how miserable she was feeling and have him comfort her. She longed to have him lie down beside her and tell her he could no longer envision his life without her, because that was definitely the way she felt about him.

Derrick emerged from the bathroom a few minutes later, switched off the light and slipped into bed. She forced herself to remain still, her back turned toward him. The heat from his body radiated toward hers and she wished for it to enclose her, dispelling the arctic chill that had encased her heart and flesh.

Suddenly, he rolled over until her back touched his chest and stomach. She nearly purred because it felt so good to be close to him, especially when a warm, strong arm encircled her waist and held her soothingly.

"Alesha?" he said, his warm breath sending shivers of desire down her spine. He softly kissed her ear. "Relax. I have no intention of trying to force myself on you."

His statement was unnecessary. They both knew he wouldn't be forcing her. She would give herself to him willingly, as she always had.

"Derrick…" She paused, not knowing what to say, or rather how to articulate what she desperately wanted from him. So she remained silent.

He pulled her closer still. "I know the confrontation with your brother was hard for you. Let me help. Let me hold you."

She couldn't believe her ears. Why was it she never knew what he was going to do next? His sincere, kind words affected her more than she would have thought possible. If only he would go a few steps further and confess his feelings.

She allowed herself to completely relax, and her hand moved slowly to rest on his as he pulled her near. She closed her eyes and he kissed her neck before resting his head by hers on the pillow. Neither made any further attempt to speak, and before she knew it, her eyes began to droop, but not before the fierce cold that had invaded her body was replaced by comforting warmth, safety and security, unlike any she had ever experienced. Soon her troubled thoughts began to dissipate, making way for restful, much-needed sleep in her husband's tender embrace.

Derrick continued to hold her. He felt the even rise and fall of her chest, indicating that she was fast asleep. Her soft form melted perfectly against his. Her fingers were entwined with his as they rested on her stomach.

Thoughts he had squelched earlier resurfaced, and again he wondered why he felt an overwhelming sense of protectiveness toward her. He pulled her nearer. She shifted slightly and then stilled. He inhaled deeply the wonderful fragrance of her hair, and he acknowledged that he truly thought of her as his wife—not just as a tool to get him elected or as an enemy to punish. He cared about her deeply—why else did the thought of her leaving him on the day their arrangement ended suddenly cause an uneasy feeling in the pit of his stomach that felt much like agony?

He shifted slowly so as not to disturb her, removing his arm from her waist to lie on his back, one hand behind his head. He stared at the ceiling. In a few short months, she had insinuated herself into his life so much that he couldn't even remember what it had been like without her or, more importantly, he didn't want to remember what it had been like without her. Before seeing her again, he had thought he was content; yet, he now knew that had been a lie. She had brought happiness and meaning into his life, which was something he admitted he had been sorely lacking for a long,

long time—since he had last been with her. She made him whole. God, she made him happy.

Alesha suddenly turned until she was lying with her head on his chest. Her arm rested across his waist, and one of her legs sprawled lazily across his.

"Derrick," she whispered contentedly before stilling.

He immediately noted how good she felt against him, as if that was where she had always belonged. Here in his arms was where he always wanted her to be. He tenderly stroked her soft hair before moving to massage her shoulder and back. She sighed comfortably and snuggled deeper into his chest. Her arm moved up to rest in the base of his neck before stilling again.

His arms pulled her closer and he smiled self-mockingly. He had been emotionally snared in a trap of his own making—one he didn't at all want to escape from. He just prayed Alesha felt the same way.

The next morning, Alesha stretched languidly in bed. She could not remember when she had experienced such a peaceful sleep. She reached out her hand in Derrick's direction, but found him gone, much to her disappointment.

She glanced at the crystal clock on the nightstand and saw it was a little after nine. He was probably long gone for the office. Rolling onto her back, she lazily pushed strands of tousled hair away from her eyes as wonderful memories of last night engulfed her.

Her husband had held and comforted her all night long. He had given of his strength unselfishly, and had demanded nothing in return from her. She would never forget how wonderful he had been to her.

She gently touched the place on her pillow where his head had lain. A smile appeared across her face. A very tangible soft spot had formed in her heart for Derrick, and there was nothing she could do to keep it from growing. Her mind tried to convince her that she was in grave danger, yet, remarkably, her heart didn't feel that way at all. She felt totally comfortable with where her relationship with Derrick was heading. She wouldn't allow anything or anyone to spoil the happiness she now felt. She laughed aloud. She was happy— Derrick made her happy and, in her heart, she knew he felt the same way about being married to her.

She lounged around in bed a few seconds longer, contemplating their future before donning a flimsy robe over her silky black gown and going downstairs. For once she would allow herself the luxury of having an unhurried breakfast— remarkably, the entire day was hers to do with as she wished. She had no political functions to attend, until tonight, and no speeches to make. She planned to have a long visit with her mother later and just indulge herself by doing absolutely nothing.

The house was quiet, confirming her suspicions that Derrick had already left. As she passed his study door, though, she heard a voice. Her heart leaped in gladness with the realization that he was still home. Without thinking, she opened the door and went in.

"Derrick, I thought you…" She stopped in midsentence as she found him sitting behind his desk, phone poised in one hand.

She was about to exit when he motioned for her to enter. She only had to wait several seconds before he wrapped up his phone conversation and stood. As he walked over to her, he noticed with satisfaction her relaxed fresh appearance and felt good that he had helped contribute to it.

"Good morning." He smiled tenderly at her.

"Good morning." Her response was given a little shyly.

"How are you feeling?" He eyed her closely.

"Much better." She paused before adding, "Thank you, Derrick."

"You're welcome, Alesha." He stared at her as if he couldn't bear to tear his eyes away.

She returned his intense gaze, wanting to say something, but not knowing what. His expressive eyes roamed over her curvaceous body through the thin negligee she wore before returning to engage hypnotically with hers. Every nerve ending in her body tingled—feeling as if he had reached out and physically explored the path that his eyes had traveled. They began to speak without saying a word, and it was very strange, very powerful and completely entrancing.

Come closer, his eyes seemed to say, and she did.

I want to touch you, her eyes responded.

Then, do it, his invited.

Her hand rose slowly, obeying her desire and his unspoken command. She trailed her fingers down his brow to his cheekbone to the side of his mouth before stopping there. Eyes that had followed the progress of her fingertips gazed into his. She moved closer, or did he? Neither really knew nor cared; it was as if they were one, yet separate, longing to be joined.

Kiss me, she spoke aloud or in her mind—she didn't know which.

I am, she heard his unspoken response as clearly as her own ragged breathing.

Her lips parted the instant his captured hers and she both fell and was drawn into his waiting embrace. Her arms were entwined tightly around his neck. His fingers raked through her tresses, pressing her lips closer to the bruising, yet caressing, force of his.

She closed her eyes and moaned in ecstasy as his strong hands roamed down her shoulders to her midback, pressing her closer. She yearned to feel his naked flesh against hers and shamelessly wished her gown and robe and his spotless charcoal-gray suit would magically disappear. She wanted him so much, and at this moment nothing else mattered, except the need they both shared for each other.

His lips devastated hers again and again. She consumed him. He didn't understand how he could want or need anyone as much as he did her. He knew if the world suddenly ended, he would be all right as long she remained right where she was, in his arms.

They both eagerly anticipated the way this passionate embrace would end, and they welcomed it. However, soon they were interrupted by a very loud cough.

It took several seconds before the sound registered in either of their minds. Reluctantly, his lips departed from hers and his eyes turned in the direction of the intrusion.

Alesha was slower to respond, first wondering why Derrick had stopped kissing her. When she opened her passion-clouded eyes and followed the direction of his gaze, she saw Cam standing in the doorway, smiling broadly. She knew the reason for Derrick's withdrawal.

"I'm sorry to interrupt. I thought you were alone, Derrick." Cam continued, smiling brightly, "Where are my manners? Good morning, Alesha."

She wished he hadn't singled her out. Pulling the folds of her flimsy robe tightly together with one hand and smoothing her tangled hair with the other, she forced herself to meet his gaze.

"Hello." Her voice was a soft whisper as she quickly lowered her embarrassed eyes.

"Is it time to leave yet?"

Derrick easily addressed his friend, and she envied his cool composure. She herself was a mass of quivering jelly.

"Just about." Cam continued grinning at them both.

"Would you two excuse me?" Alesha shot Derrick a quick

glance before she nearly ran from the room and up the stairs to the safety of their bedroom.

"Well, well, well." Cam sat on the side of Derrick's desk.

"Don't start, Cameron." Derrick's eyes darted regretfully to Alesha's hastily retreating back.

"Have you told Alesha how you feel?"

"Not that it's any of your business, but no."

"Why not?"

"Cam, our relationship is complicated."

"Made so by the both of you." He treated Derrick to an exaggerated wink before standing. "Derrick, just tell her! From what I saw, she feels the same way about you."

"You think so?" He walked from behind his desk and scratched his chin.

"Oh, yeah, I think so." He patted his shoulder. "Make it work, man, or you'll regret it."

"Let's go." Derrick picked up his briefcase and preceded him out without answering, though his expression was very thoughtful.

Chapter 12

Alone in their bedroom, Alesha sat on the bed, smiling secretively to herself while replaying the last kiss Derrick and she had shared, fantasizing about the different ending both had wanted before Cam had interrupted them. She gingerly touched her lips and jumped when the phone rang. Sighing, she leaned over to pick up the handset.

"Hello."

"Hi, it's Derrick."

She nearly dropped the phone upon hearing his warm, husky voice. Had he somehow known she was thinking about him? Her insides warmed to know he had been thinking of her.

"Derrick."

There was an uncomfortable pause, each waiting for the other to speak. She had so much she wanted to say, yet she didn't know where to begin.

"What do you have planned for the day?" He asked the question just to hear her voice.

"Well, for a change, my schedule is free." She laughed a little nervously. "I'm probably going to visit Mom."

"That's good. She'll be glad to see you. Give her my best."

"I will."

After a few seconds, he added, "I called to remind you about dinner tonight."

"Thanks, I remember." She chewed on her lower lip thoughtfully.

"Could you make sure my tux is back from the cleaners?"

"Of course, I'll be happy to." She smiled, closing her eyes and picturing his handsome face. "Did you finish your speech?" That was her roundabout way of bringing the conversation back to last night.

"No, but I will at the office." He paused. "I'm sorry Cam walked in on us." He came to the real purpose for his call.

She opened her eyes and was suddenly glad he couldn't see her. Was he apologizing for her embarrassment, or because they had been unable to finish what they had started?

"So was I," she said, realizing how her voice sounded. She quickly added, "What I mean is…"

"I know what you meant."

She could hear the smile in his voice and embarrassment kept her from responding. She wished he was with her now so that they could… She shook her head forcefully, forestalling completion of that thought.

"Well, I'll see you tonight around six."

"Derrick?" She stalled, realizing he was about to hang up.

"Yes?" He waited.

"I—I'll see you tonight. Have a good day." She didn't have anything else to say—she simply didn't want to let him go.

"Tonight," he echoed before ending the call.

She slowly replaced the phone in its cradle. Smiling brightly, she entered the bathroom to prepare for her day.

A short while later, Alesha was still smiling when she sat down beside her mom on the sofa. "How have you been?"

"I've been fine, but I want to hear about you and Derrick. How are the two of you doing?" She smiled.

"Wonderfully, though we're both very busy. I was lucky to have today free." Alesha placed an affectionate kiss on her mother's cheek.

"I'm glad you did." Barbara smiled, adding approvingly, "Derrick is a very nice man. I'm glad you found him."

"Yes, so am I." Her admission came out breathless.

"I've enjoyed our talks."

"Your talks?" Alesha frowned.

"Yes, dear. He calls several times a week and stops by at least once a week."

Her mother's words floored her. Did Derrick really keep in such close contact with her? If so, why?

"He does?"

"Of course. Didn't you know?"

"He didn't mention it. I suppose it slipped his mind."

"You're probably right." Her mother nodded in agreement. "I've told him not to try to fit me into his busy schedule, but he doesn't listen."

"That's Derrick for you." Alesha silently pondered her mother's words.

"A mother couldn't ask for a better son-in-law or husband for her only daughter. He's such a good man."

"Yes, he is, Mom." Alesha smiled contemplatively.

"When are you two going to make me a Big Momma?"

"Momma!" A hand flew to her mouth in shock.

"What?" Barbara laughed at her. "You're not getting any younger and neither am I."

"We've only been married a few months."

She winked conspiratorially. "That's all it takes."

"I know, but let us get used to being married first, okay?"

"What's there to get used to?" Barbara persisted. "That's what's wrong with young people these days—you think you have all the time in the world. Believe me, time waits for no one."

"I know that, but—" she paused as an unnerving thought formed in her mind "—you haven't talked to Derrick about this, have you?"

"Of course not, dear. I was saving my pleading for you."

"Good."

Alesha visibly relaxed. She would have been mortified if her mother and husband had been discussing something so intimate.

"Well?"

"Momma, let me enjoy being a newlywed for a while."

Barbara sighed. "Oh, all right. As long as you remember what I said about running out of time."

"I'll remember."

"Good." Barbara beamed. "I can't wait."

Alesha smiled at her mother indulgently, but wisely remained silent as, for the first time, she fantasized about having Derrick's baby. At the thought of her husband, her heart began to flutter erratically.

She had become so accustomed to being his wife in every sense of the word, even before he had slipped the wedding ring on her finger. And now her mother had planted the idea of having his child, a thought that filled her with joy. How would he react? she wondered.

He cared for her. If she had any doubt about that, last night had erased it. The evolution of their marriage had been natural and inevitable. She had wanted him since that first kiss in his office months ago. She had wanted him every day for the past two years, though she had fought like hell against acknowledging that truth. She smiled at her mother. Life was funny and surprising. She only prayed it would give her what she wanted most—Derrick's heart.

That night, Alesha was dressed in a black, figure-hugging, sleeveless slip dress with a slight train at the back. She wore opera-length black satin gloves. A double-strand pearl-and-diamond bracelet rested on her left gloved wrist, and teardrop pearl-and-diamond earrings dangled from her ears. Her hair was swept loosely up with curls escaping, caressing her neck. A few loose tendrils were flung carelessly over her right eye.

She had told Derrick she was wearing her hair as a compromise—wanting to wear it up, but knowing he preferred it loose. He had laughed at her words, though she had known her explanation had pleased him.

Derrick was dressed in a crisp-white dinner jacket and shirt, and black slacks. He walked out of his dressing room attempting to fasten his tie. Alesha laughed at his predicament and brushed his fingers away.

"Here, let me do it." She picked up the material and tied it perfectly.

She raised her eyes and found him staring at her with the strangest expression. Impulsively, he placed a feathery kiss on her lips, but moved away suddenly to inspect her handiwork in the mirror.

"Thanks."

"You're welcome." She smiled slightly, wishing their kiss had not been so brief or so unsatisfying.

"You look exquisite."

She blushed as his piercing eyes swept over her. It was amazing how a mere look from Derrick could suck the air from her lungs.

"Thank you." After studying his appearance, she added, "You look pretty good yourself."

He smiled at her words and unexpectedly asked, "How did your visit go with your mother?"

"Fine." She walked past him to freshen up her lipstick.

"I'm glad." He smiled as he walked over to stand beside her, searching the dresser top for his cuff links.

She picked up a bottle of perfume and lightly sprayed her bare neck. Derrick inhaled the sensuous scent deeply and their eyes met again in the mirror. Her chest rose rapidly and his eyes darted to her neck. She felt breathless, as if his hands were caressing her, silently wishing they were. She lowered the perfume with one hand and picked up a double-strand pearl-and-diamond necklace with the other, her eyes never leaving his in the mirror.

He took the necklace from her fingers and placed it around her neck before fastening it. His fingers lingered unnecessarily long on her soft flesh. There was no denying what they both wanted.

To remove temptation, he turned and walked over to the bed and sat down. He put on his black shoes. She watched him through the mirror, wondering why he hadn't given in to an impulse she knew they both had shared. He raised his head and caught her questioning gaze before she quickly looked away.

"Mom asked about you." She spoke primarily to have something to say.

"That was nice of her." He stood and placed a handkerchief inside the pocket of his dinner jacket.

"She said something that surprised me." She walked over to where he stood, placing her hand on his strong arm while she slipped into her black pumps.

"What was that?" He looked at her curiously as she straightened to face him.

"That you keep in regular contact with her." She watched him closely.

"So?" He wondered where this was leading.

"So, why haven't you ever mentioned it to me?"

His eyebrows arched slightly and he stepped away to grab his keys off the nightstand. "I wasn't aware I had to. I happen to like Barbara and I care about how she's doing. Do you have a problem with that?"

"No, not at all." She was warmed by his words. "I was just surprised you hadn't said anything about it to me."

He stared at her strangely. "We'd better get going." He picked up her faux-mink black stole and helped her into it.

"I need to put the finishing touches on my makeup. Why don't you bring the car around?"

"You look beautiful." He kissed her cheek before opening the door. "But go ahead and finish your war paint and I'll meet you downstairs."

"Okay."

He quickly descended the stairs and opened the front door, finding Diana loitering there. He didn't bother to hide his displeasure. Damn, what now?

"Diana, what are you doing here?"

"May I come in?"

"No. Alesha and I are on our way out."

"I need to speak with you, darling."

She walked past him into the foyer. He reluctantly closed the door and turned to face her.

"First of all, I'm not your darling and, second, I don't have time to waste on you—now or ever."

"Can we go into your study?"

"No."

Alesha's footsteps faltered and stopped at the top of the stairs as Derrick's voice and a female one she recognized as Diana's wafted up to her. What was she doing here?

"What do you want?"

"I want you to take me back."

"Have you lost your mind?" He looked at her as if she had. "I'm married."

"You don't love her," Diana scoffed.

"And I suppose you think I love you?" At her silence he continued, "Diana, why would I want you back and, more importantly, why would you want me? I never loved you—I made no pretense about that."

Her smile faltered. "That's not true."

"Still delusional, I see." He laughed. "You didn't want a husband. You wanted a puppy dog to follow you around while you embellished your career—something I was never going to be. I wasn't ambitious enough for you then, but now that I have a shot at being a U.S. Senator, I look better in your eyes, is that it?"

"I've realized we want the same things, Derrick. I could help you become the best senator and you could help my lobbying firm once you get in office."

He chuckled as her motives were finally revealed. "Is that what this is all about—the powerful, influential people I will meet once I'm in the Senate? People you think can further your career?"

"Our careers, Derrick." Her eyes pleaded with his. "I can help you in ways she never could!"

"I doubt that."

"Derrick." Her red nails dug into his arm. "Don't be a fool!"

"I was once." His eyes narrowed as he removed her hand. "But never again."

"I'll go to the press."

He raised an eyebrow. "With what? A lame exposé of how I married you on the rebound, quickly realized my mistake and happily remedied it, but not before I felt soiled by you?"

At the top of the stairs, Alesha watched and listened to the exchange with keen interest. She learned more as an observer than she ever could have from questioning Derrick about his ex. This woman had nerve and a half! Angela was right—she was a hussy! Having heard enough, she walked down the stairs, ready for battle.

"You know it's sisters like you who give other sisters a bad name."

"Amen!" Derrick shook his head in agreement.

"Is that right?" Diana turned hateful eyes in her direction as Alesha walked over to stand by Derrick.

"Yes, that's right," Alesha said, placing a possessive hand on her husband's arm. "I was threatened by you, but now I see how silly I was."

"Really?" Diana scowled.

"Yes." Alesha laughed. "You're pathetic."

"Listen, you little…"

"I'm Mrs. Derrick Chandler." She slowly enunciated every word and smiled at Derrick when he placed his arm supportively around her waist. "That's something you'll never be again."

"She certainly won't," Derrick vowed.

"I'll be the one by Derrick's side when he takes his place in congress, not you. You had your chance and you blew it. He doesn't want you. How many ways does he have to say that before it sinks in?"

She'd had her fill of this insufferable woman! Despite the way their marriage had begun, she and Derrick were married. He was hers and she had no intention of giving him up, especially not to the likes of this woman!

"Diana, I don't know what story you think you have to sell to the press, but go ahead and sell it to the highest bidder."

"You don't mean that."

"Don't I?" He pulled Alesha closer. "I have what I want and need right here in my arms and there's nothing you can do to take it away."

"Nothing at all," Alesha firmly chimed in.

"If you want to ruin your own career by spreading malicious lies about our brief, unpleasant dalliance, then go ahead. But knowing how ambitious you are, I don't think you will."

"Now that you've embarrassed yourself beyond compare, will you do us the pleasure of leaving our home and never returning?" Alesha smiled brightly.

"Gladly." Diana's eyes shot daggers at them both. "You two deserve each other!"

"See, darling? I think she finally got the message."

To twist the knife further, Alesha turned into his arms and kissed Derrick. They heard heels clicking and a door slamming, and when they pulled apart, she was gone.

"Good riddance!" Derrick vowed. "The audacity of that woman!"

"She is a brassy one." Alesha laughed, wiping lipstick from his mouth with her fingers. "What did you ever see in her?"

He joined her laughter. "I don't know. She caught me at a low point and I foolishly thought she could help me forget."

"Me?"

"Yes. What an idiot I was." He laughed at himself. "She's nothing like you, which, I guess, was her appeal."

She sobered at his admission. "Derrick, I'm sorry."

"You don't have anything to be sorry about."

"Yes, I do." She closed her eyes briefly and came to a decision. "I want to tell you why I pushed you away two years ago. Everything."

"Now?" He brushed a stray strand of hair out of her troubled eyes.

"Yes, it's about time. Don't you think?"

She was tired of keeping secrets from him, of all people. She needed to be completely honest with him. He deserved it.

"It can wait."

"No. I've held this in long enough. You have been so wonderful to me. You deserve the truth, if you still want to hear it." She placed her palms on his chest and waited for his response.

"I do." He covered one of her hands with his.

She took a deep breath and then released it. "First of all, what I said at your country house after the wedding about my feelings for you frightening me was true."

"I felt the same way." His admission made it easier for her to proceed.

"Do you remember when we were dating before and you wanted me to meet Cam?" She focused her attention on a pearl-white button on his shirtfront.

"Of course. We were going to have dinner, but you had to cancel."

"I was there at the restaurant." She tilted her head until her eyes meet his.

"You were?"

"Yes. I was coming out of the ladies' room. You and Cam had your backs to me and I overheard you telling him that you were so happy to be in a relationship with someone who didn't want anything from you. Someone who wasn't carrying around a lot of excess baggage, or who had a mountain of problems she expected you to miraculously fix." She related his words verbatim.

"Alesha, I didn't mean…" Her fingers on his lips silenced him.

"No, it's all right." She removed her fingers from his mouth to rest on his jaw. "I had just learned that morning that Momma had a life-threatening heart condition—one that was going to require surgery and long rehabilitation."

"Oh, God!" He finally had the missing piece of the puzzle. "She seems so healthy."

"She's been doing great since her surgeries."

"Thank God for that."

"Robert and I wanted her to have the best doctors."

"Of course you did."

"I ended up emptying my savings and other bank accounts and selling what good jewelry I had and my car. Robert did the same and got a second job, but it still wasn't enough. Even after insurance and taking out loans, it left us with huge bills, but about six months ago, she had a slight relapse and her doctor wanted her to see a specialist—one who wouldn't consult on her case unless we came up with our share of the money upfront, and that's why Robert took your money."

He paused before asking, "Why didn't you tell me?"

She shrugged. "I was going to the day we met again, but…"

He sighed. "But I said I didn't care."

"Yes."

"I lied. I did and I do care."

"Thank you for saying that."

"I mean it. Barbara is a special lady."

"She's everything to Bobby and me."

"I know. I'll apologize to him."

"You don't have to do that."

"Yes, I do." His eyes grew intense. "Who is Kevin? Obviously, he wasn't your lover as you led me to believe."

"No." She shook her head. "He's the brother of a friend. He came up to see his sister for the weekend, but she was out of town, so I let him sleep on my sofa. He's like a brother to me."

"Why did you let me think something else?"

"Because I had tried everything to get you to accept my decision to end things between us, and you wouldn't do it. I didn't plan for you to see me and Kevin the way you did— me dressed in a robe and him only in shorts, both obviously fresh out of the shower. The opportunity just presented itself and I shamelessly took advantage of it." She paused. "I knew what it looked like, I knew what you thought and I let you believe we were lovers because I knew that would end things between us once and for all. It hurt too much to keep seeing you and speaking to you on the phone—telling you I didn't want a relationship with you when the truth was that was all I did want, but couldn't have at that time."

"Why didn't you come to me once things were somewhat resolved?"

"How could I after the horrible way we parted?" She shrugged helplessly. "I honestly didn't think you would want to see me again and I didn't want to face your contempt."

Her eyes implored him to understand her actions and the reasons behind them. His thumbs lightly stroked her cheeks and he smiled at her tenderly. His mind sorted through dozens of questions that suddenly seemed meaningless. He had just received the answers to the most important questions.

"Oh, Alesha." He sighed her name. "So there never was anyone else?"

"Never." She shook her head. "I was just so overwhelmed, but now my reasons for pushing you away seem so trivial and stupid."

"You always wanted me?" He skipped to the heart of the matter—the only question he needed answered.

"Always," she agreed without hesitation.

Neither of them spoke for a long time. They simply stared

into each other's eyes, silently telegraphing secret messages of regret, sorrow—and hope.

"It's in the past. Let's leave it there and go forward," he finally suggested.

"That sounds good."

His thumb brushed away a tear that escaped from the corner of her eye. He smiled slightly and kissed her—the gentlest, softest kiss she had ever experienced—and it melted her soul and her heart. He was such an enigma to her. She never knew what he was going to do or say, yet he always seemed to do and say the right thing.

"It hurt me more than I thought anything could when you suddenly and completely shut me out of your life." He tenderly fingered her hair. "It infuriated me that you never gave us a fighting chance."

"I couldn't. You sucked up all the oxygen until I didn't have anything left. Bottom line—my mother needed me and I didn't have the time, inclination or strength to be in a relationship with you, no matter how much I wanted to."

"Did you want to?"

"Yes. In the short time we dated, I felt alive as I never had before."

"Your rejection sent me headlong into a disastrous relationship with a woman I should never have given the time of day."

"Your marriage to Diana."

"Legally." He smiled ruefully. "But what I had with her was never a marriage."

"I was so jealous when you told me about her."

"Why?"

She took a deep breath before admitting, "Because she was your wife, a wife you *wanted* to marry."

"We were married, Alesha, but she was never my wife—not like you."

"I'm just a means to an end."

He frowned. "Do you honestly believe that, still?"

"I don't want to."

"You're my wife, Alesha." His hands framed her face. "That's how I think of you."

"And you're my husband." She paused before asking, "Do you want to stay married to me, Derrick?"

"Do you?"

They smiled at each other tenderly, without answering verbally. She suddenly knew she could never live without him—just as she knew she had fallen helplessly, irrevocably in love with him twice. After all the years of soul-searching she had done, that revelation came as naturally and effortlessly to her as breathing did. For a moment, she thought that she had spoken her feelings out loud, because Derrick's expression shifted to one of total gentleness and understanding. Did she imagine it, or was there a reciprocal wonderment in his eyes as if he, too, had come to the same conclusion?

Chapter 13

At the party, both Derrick and Alesha tried to put the unpleasant scene with Diana out of their minds. They were on the dance floor. Her head lay on Derrick's shoulder, eyes closed. One hand rested on his opposite shoulder, while the other was clasped in his warm hand, close to her face as they swayed to the soft music. His head rested against her hair as he held her close.

"Are you okay?" Derrick's question forced Alesha to lift her head.

"Yes, I'm fine." She stared at him adoringly. More than anything, she wanted to feel his lips on hers.

His eyes shifted to her moist lips, reading her mind, and then moved back to her beautiful face. "We can leave if you want to."

"This is important to you—we can stay." Then at his continued look of concern, she added, "Really, I'm fine."

He gave in to temptation then and grazed her lips with his. He allowed himself to lightly caress her mouth for a few seconds, before he pulled away—knowing if he didn't, things would get embarrassing.

She replaced her head on his shoulder, instinctively knowing why he had ended their brief kiss. Disentangling her hand from his, she slid her hand up his shoulder until both her arms encircled his neck. His hands moved from her waist to her lower back, holding her closer still as they continued to dance.

She closed her eyes again, allowing herself to escape. It felt so good to be in his arms. She didn't want to be anywhere else, except where she was, and she knew that neither did he. This was where she was meant to be—forever.

He wished he had her home right now, because he would make passionate love to her—he would make her forget all the pain she had experienced. He was determined to erase the past hurts and dissolve the years they had spent without each other. In his arms, he would make her feel nothing except complete ecstasy.

Unfortunately, the song ended too quickly, and they reluctantly left each other's arms and walked off the dance floor hand in hand, only to find Cam curiously watching them both. As they approached, Derrick's eyes silently warned him not to make any flippant comments.

"Senator Hatcher wants to speak with you, Derrick," Cam informed him as they reached his side.

"Do you want me to come with you?"

Alesha placed her hand on his arm as she stared at him lovingly. The look she gave him almost took his breath away.

"No, I'll be back shortly. Stay here and try to keep Cam out of trouble, will you?" His eyes darted to his friend.

"I'll try." She smiled. He kissed her softly before walking away.

"Where's Mary?" she asked, referring to Cam's date.

"Oh, she's in the ladies room or somewhere." Cam

seemed to have little interest in his date's whereabouts. "Are you enjoying yourself tonight?"

"I am."

"I know these functions can be very boring, but…"

"They're a necessary evil." She completed the sentence for him with a knowing wink.

"I see you've heard that from time to time."

"Once or twice." She smiled.

Cam laughed. "Derrick can be a workhorse when it comes to his career, but he's also very kind and giving. Of course, you know that, don't you?"

"He's a very complex man." She cautiously eyed him over the rim of her glass.

"Not really, not once you understand his motivations. I hope you'll try to."

"Why is that so important to you?"

"He's my friend—my best friend. I want him to be happy, and you make him happy."

"What about Diana?"

He grimaced. "Please! She wouldn't know how to think about someone else if her life depended on it!"

"Have you seen her since she returned to town?"

"No, and God willing I will be spared that unpleasantness."

She laughed. "You don't like her very much, do you?"

"Nope." He shook his head emphatically. "And I never did."

"Why?"

"Because she is, was and always will be a user."

"You're right about that."

He frowned. "What is she trying to pull?"

"Oh, nothing." Alesha shook her head. "She doesn't matter."

"I'm glad to hear you say that."

"Why?"

"Because I know she came back into town to try to cause trouble for you and Derrick."

"She did, but she can't." Alesha smiled. "We won't let her."

"I think Diana has met her match."

She smiled secretively. "I think she knows that now."

"Derrick would have my hide if he knew I was saying this to you." Cam glanced away briefly to make sure his friend was nowhere to be seen.

"But?"

"But I'm going to say it anyway. You're good for him. As I told him this morning, I don't understand why the two of you won't admit your marriage is real."

"You told him that?" Her face registered surprise and gratitude.

"I did."

"What was his response?"

"What's yours?" he quickly countered.

"Well, I…" She was interrupted by Derrick as he joined them, placing a possessive arm around her waist.

"What were you two so engrossed in?" He eyed them both closely.

"Your campaign. What else?" Cam smiled.

Alesha shot him a grateful look. Derrick noted the quick exchange between them and made a mental note to find out what mischief Cam had been up to in his absence.

Hours later when they entered their bedroom, Derrick helped her off with her stole, placing it on a nearby chair. He reached for the light, but Alesha's hand prevented him from flipping the switch on. Her hand traveled up his muscled arm to his shoulder, coming to rest behind his head as she moved closer to him. She pulled his face toward hers as she placed a lingering kiss on his lips.

She kissed him slowly, enjoying every second, every movement of their lips against each other's. His hands caressed her waist as she continued to astonish and delight him with her forwardness. When she slowly withdrew her lips from his, he stared at her expectantly, yet made no move toward her—leaving the outcome in her hands.

Her fingers deftly unfastened his tie before moving to unbutton his shirt, sliding it and the jacket simultaneously from his broad shoulders. As her fingers lightly touched the hair on his chest, he sucked in his breath quickly, as if the contact burned him. She moved closer to his hard body and her hands splayed across his muscled back as her lips captured his once again.

He couldn't believe this was happening. Alesha was initiating intimacy between them. He had longed for this moment for what seemed like forever. He knew tonight was going to be special beyond compare.

"Will you undo my necklace?" Her question was posed softly.

His lips captured hers briefly, promising a much more satisfying union, before he walked behind her. She raised her hair out of the way as his fingers quickly unclasped her necklace. He kissed her neck, and she reached her gloved hand up behind her to caress the side of his face before moving to his nape, holding him closer. Then she turned around in his arms. He unclasped the bracelet on her wrist. Her hand still held his face—she reluctantly released him to remove one glove and then the other, before placing her hands on his chest.

"Unzip my dress."

He smiled at her words, and readily did as she gently commanded, sliding his hands beneath the material at her back, pulling her closer as the dress fell to the floor. Their lips played with each other's, nipping, caressing briefly and moving away, his fingers unclasped her hair, freeing the silky tresses, running his fingers slowly through it.

"You've wanted to do that all night, haven't you?" she asked.

He returned her smile tenderly before admitting, "Yes. Just as I've wanted to do this." His lips attacked hers with such ferocity she felt as if she were being eaten alive. The passionate mating of their lips caused an answering response in their bodies as they pressed closer.

Her hands clutched at his shoulders, arching against his hard, unbending frame. His hands roamed down her bare back to her hips, pressing her tighter against him as he greedily took what she so freely offered. Soon, however, they knew this was not enough—they needed more, much more.

"Derrick, make love to me. I need you. How I want you."

She was going for broke tonight—she was tired of hiding her feelings. One way or another, she would find out what she meant to him and she would tell him what he meant to her.

He bent and scooped her up in his arms. Walking over to the bed, he laid her down on it before following her with his own body. They kissed passionately as her hands trailed down his flat, hard stomach to his belt buckle, urgently undoing it before unzipping his pants. She touched his skin, softly at first and then more fervently. He was on fire and becoming more inflamed with her every caress.

She watched the expressions race across his face at her ardent manipulations. She squeezed him intimately until his hand covered hers, ending her sweet torture. She tried unsuccessfully to elude his grasp and when he refused to release her, she turned questioning eyes to the fiery depths of his.

"Don't you want me to touch you?" She bit his chin softly.

He closed his eyes shortly before opening them again and hissing, "Yes!"

"Then why are you stopping me?" Her lips traced his jawline, her hand escaping from his, continuing her tantalizing exploration.

"Because if you don't stop, I'm going to go insane." His promise was growled as his lips ardently nipped at hers.

"Good." She sighed between caresses. "I don't want you to be in control. I want you to lose yourself in me as I am in you."

His eyes grew dark at her words as his hands slid down her throat to her smooth shoulders. His lips replaced his hands, trailing across her satiny skin, igniting a fire within that she knew would soon consume them both.

"Make me yours, Derrick. Travel with me to that special place in the universe only we two can occupy together."

She didn't need to ask twice. His mouth devastated hers and she participated eagerly in their passionate, all-consuming kisses. When his lips lifted from hers, their now-naked limbs pressed closely together.

He rasped, "I will. Right now."

"I want you so much that it hurts," she groaned without hesitation.

"Alesha!" He nearly exploded as her wandering hand enfolded and caressed him.

"Do you want me?"

"Yes, more than you know."

"Then take me, darling. Make me yours forever." She arched against his hard body.

His fingers caressed her hair, roughly pulling her lips back to his. She was here in his arms, saying things he had longed to hear her say, responding to him unashamedly, feeling free to touch him.

His hands descended her sides to her hips, pressing her closer as he joined his body to hers without further hesitation. They melted together perfectly—proof that they had been made for each other. She shivered uncontrollably against his throbbing body. She had said she wanted no control and she received none. He claimed her body and heart and she willingly gave him everything she had, and received all in return.

His lips left hers and she bit into his strong shoulder, simultaneously raking her nails down his torso. His body continued to scorch hers. They belonged to each other—nothing was held back by either of them. Their bodies made rapturous music, and after several long, passion-filled hours, the unique love song they had created neared its inevitable, unforgettable conclusion.

They soared higher on wings of pure, unselfish love. He moaned hoarsely and she groaned in ecstasy as waves of intense pleasure cascaded through their souls. It was a total union of hearts and souls—this time, they truly did break the barrier of their bodies as they combined themselves into one life force. He loved her, and she loved him totally without reserve. All pretense of anything else was stripped away. They both knew nothing had ever been, or would ever be, so right again.

Much later, she was nearly sleeping, head resting on Derrick's chest. Her fingers were entwined with his. She sighed in contentment—everything was perfect. Finally, she knew she had all she would ever need—right here in Derrick's arms.

He had never felt as close to anyone as he did now. He belonged to her with every fiber of his being, with all that he possessed. God, he adored her. He finally admitted to himself what he had long felt. How could he possibly deny it?

"You know, Cam has told me on more than one occasion that we should try to make our marriage work." His fingers trailed up and down the satiny skin of her back.

"He told me the same thing tonight." She lifted her head to stare at him lovingly.

"What did you tell him?"

"Nothing, you interrupted us." She smiled.

"Do you want our marriage to work?" He held his breath as he waited for her answer—the most important answer he would ever receive in his life.

"Our marriage does work." She kissed his chest before raising her eyes to meet his again. "We work. I'm your wife and you're my husband. There's nothing false about that, or the fact that I love you more than I thought I could ever love anyone." She finally admitted what had been in her heart for a long time.

He smiled at her as tenderly as she had ever seen and let out a breath that she realized he had been holding expectantly. "I love you, too, very much."

"Really?" She kissed his lips lightly.

"Yes. Didn't you know?" He ran fingers through her tousled hair.

"I hoped."

"So did I." He pulled her head down to his to engage in a passionate, loving kiss. "Alesha…" he whispered against her lips.

"Hmm?" She tried to bring his mouth back to hers, but when he resisted, she opened dreamy eyes to stare into the serious depths of his. "What's wrong?"

"I'm sorry." His solemn words startled her.

"For what?" She traced his furrowed brow with her fingers.

"For forcing you into this marriage." He painfully articulated the guilt that had plagued him for months.

"Derrick, you didn't force me—I always had a choice."

"Yes, but I took advantage…" Her fingers on his lips forestalled his words.

"Shh. I'm where I want to be—I don't care how I got here. I only care that I did get here—that we got here together, finally."

"Really?" He searched her eyes.

"Really." She nodded, allowing every ounce of love she felt for him to shine in her eyes, for him to see. "Why didn't you tell me you loved me sooner?"

He smiled sheepishly. "I was waiting for you to say it."

"Oh, yeah." She laughed softly. "Well, I guess I can't blame you for that."

"I love you so much." He made up for lost time. "I have from the first moment I saw you."

"I love you, too. With all my heart."

Loving fingers caressed her face. His mouth captured hers, ending any response she had been about to make. She wiggled on top of him and stretched her soft body out the length of his. Their legs entangled intimately.

After reluctantly releasing her lips, he groaned, "You have sapped all my energy, but I want you again and again."

"Then take me, darling, as many times as you want me. I'm yours."

"Mine?" His hands roamed down her bare back.

"Completely." She smiled. "Forever."

Their mouths fused together, sealing their promise of eternal love with an endless kiss.

A week later, they were at her mother's, enjoying the unseasonably warm weather with an impromptu backyard barbecue.

"Hey, you guys, is it done yet?"

"In a minute." Derrick laughed at his wife. "You sure have been eating a lot lately."

"Love does wonders for my appetite."

"Mine, too." He bobbed his eyes at her.

"Derrick!"

He and Robert laughed before turning back to the grill. In Barbara's honor, they were having a heart-healthy meal consisting of grilled salmon and vegetables.

Barbara glanced toward the two men. "I'm so glad Robert is warming up to Derrick."

Alesha smiled. "So am I."

"He was having trouble letting his little sister go, but now he knows you're in good hands."

"I definitely am."

"You're happy," her mother responded.

"Deliriously." She reached across the table and squeezed her hand. "Can something so wonderful possibly last?"

"It did with your father and me until the day he died."

"That's what I want with Derrick."

"Then that's what you'll have," Barbara promised. "You two are perfect together."

Robert and Derrick laughed as they fought back flames and quickly removed food from the grill.

"I don't think I've ever seen Alesha happier and I have you to thank for that."

Derrick smiled. "I should be thanking you."

"Why?"

"You brought us back together again and I will forever be in your debt. I know what my life was without her and I never want to experience that pain again."

"You love her." Robert nodded in approval.

"With all my heart."

"I'm happy for you both, Derrick."

"Thanks, Robert. That means a lot coming from you."

"Just keep her happy."

"Always."

"Derrick," he slowly began. "I'm sorry I embezzled from your campaign. I'll pay you back."

"No." He shook his head. "Thank you for your apology, but I don't want your money."

Robert frowned. "Why not?"

"Alesha told me why you took it. I'm a part of this family now and I love Barbara, too."

"Thanks." Robert smiled. "Welcome to the family."

Derrick returned his smile. "Thank you."

They were laughing when they carried the food over to the table. Derrick bent down and kissed his wife briefly before sitting down next to Barbara.

"Here you are." Robert placed a platter of grilled corn on the cob next to the salmon.

"Mmm…" Alesha's eyes sparkled. "It smells and looks wonderful!"

Barbara eyed the healthy feast cautiously. "It does look good, but what I wouldn't give for a plate of ribs!"

"When you taste this, you'll forget all about greasy ribs," Derrick promised, kissing her cheek.

"If you say so, dear." She patted his hand.

"Momma, behave yourself," Alesha chided.

"Mom, you know how bossy she is," Robert said sympathetically.

"She's perfect," Derrick said, coming to his wife's defense.

"Thank you, darling." She blew him a kiss. "I love you."

"And I love you."

Barbara smiled approvingly. "Aren't they cute, Robert?"

He chuckled. "Adorable."

"Just you wait—your turn will come." Alesha wagged her finger at him.

"Let's eat." Robert wisely avoided responding to her prediction.

Everyone laughed and all set about filling their plates. Above the laughter and good-natured banter, Derrick and Alesha's eyes met and held. They smiled at each other secretively. There was no need for words. She loved and needed him—how wonderful to know that he felt the same way about her. All her life, she had searched for this and now it was finally hers. She was so glad to know that her mother was right—they were perfect for each other.

Epilogue

It was the middle of November and Derrick and Alesha would be celebrating their one-year anniversary in two weeks. She reclined against the soft back of the sofa, remote in her hand as she again proudly watched her husband giving his senatorial victory speech. A fire crackled comfortingly as Derrick sat beside her, his ear and hands pressed to her huge stomach, anticipating some sign of activity from their unborn child.

"Sweetheart," he said, leaning against her stomach. "Aren't you tired of watching this?"

"No, and you're not, either."

"I can't believe a year has passed. I'm a senator and you're about to give birth to our first child." He repositioned his ear on her stomach.

"I know what you mean." She smiled down at him.

He lifted his head to stare at her adoringly. He looked just like a kid on Christmas Day. She laughed out loud at the anxious expression in his eyes.

"What?"

"You look so cute!" Her smile widened at his scowl.

He sat up, hands still placed gingerly on her huge stomach and indignantly replied, "Cute? I am not cute."

"Oh, yes, you are, darling." She laughed, kissing his nose softly. "Did you feel that?" She beamed as the baby kicked.

"Yes, yes, I did."

He moved his fingers around to see if he could capture that amazing evidence of life growing within her. Her hands covered his as both waited, and another and yet another kick came.

"Our son or daughter is certainly active tonight."

"Yes, he or she is." His fingers lightly caressed her swollen stomach. "Are you in any pain?"

"No."

"Do you think we should get going to the hospital?" He sat up and watched her anxiously.

"No, sweetheart. I haven't had a contraction for a while. I think we still have time." She tried unsuccessfully to soothe his frayed nerves.

"I think we should go now—just in case."

"Derrick, I'll know when it's time to go." She stroked his furrowed brow.

"Well, if you're sure…"

"I am." Trying to get his mind off her impending labor, she replied, "Life is so funny."

"In what way?"

"Well, look at us—two people who were sworn enemies a short time ago, who are now totally in love with each other and anticipating the birth of our child."

"I never considered you an enemy." His hands still wandered over her huge stomach.

"But, darling, I considered you mine." She smiled.

"Really?"

She laughed. "Well, maybe for all of a second."

"I am crushed!"

"No, you're not." Her hand caressed his jaw.

"No, I'm not." He moved closer to her. "But I'm not your adversary anymore, am I?" His lips gravitated to within mere inches of hers.

"Of course not. You're my best friend, the love of my life. In fact, I love you more than life itself." She sighed before his lips closed over hers in a warm kiss. "I'm so happy."

"I'm going to make sure you stay that way." He kissed her again, lingering on her lips this time.

"I will as long as I have you." She snuggled contentedly, placing his head in the crook of her neck.

"You have me forever." They were silent for a while before he spoke again. "Sweetheart, do you ever think of returning to nursing?"

"No. Why?" She wondered where that question had come from.

"I just want you to be content, and I know how much your career means to you." He turned his head to stare at her profile intensely.

"*Meant* to me," she quickly corrected. "I have all I want and need right here in this room."

"Are you sure?"

"Definitely, but I love you for asking." She smiled.

"I'd do anything to make you happy."

"You have and you do."

He repositioned his head in her neck, taking love bites out of her soft flesh. "Gimme a kiss."

"My pleasure." She turned her head ever so lightly, bringing her lips into contact with his. Before their kiss could deepen, though, she winced in pain. "Ouch!"

Immediately his head lifted from her shoulder, concern

and apprehension emanating from every aspect of his being. "Another contraction?"

"Yes." She began to pant slightly. "How long has it been since the last one?"

"About fifteen minutes." He nervously glanced at his watch.

They both looked at each other, and she could tell he was quickly beginning to panic. "Derrick, calm down. Women have babies every day."

"Not my wife!" He jumped up and anxiously began pacing to and fro, unable to decide what to do first. "Can you walk? Do I need to carry you?"

Between the pain and panting breaths, she began to laugh hysterically, unable to stop herself. He was so funny!

"Derrick! Derrick, relax, baby," she pleaded through giggles.

He finally decided on a course of action, running to grab her already packed suitcase. Then he picked up both of their coats and his car keys before rushing back to the sofa where she sat doubled over in pain and laughter.

"It's not nice to laugh at your newest senator." He held out his hands to help her to her feet.

"If your constituents could see you now." She kissed his cheek gently as he pulled her upright. "Don't forget to call Momma and Robert."

"I'll call from the car."

He placed her coat around her shoulders before leading her slowly, yet urgently, to the door. She fought against another bout of laughter as she glanced at his tense, terrified expression.

"I love you." She suddenly stopped, smiled and kissed his lips thoroughly and, she hoped, comfortingly.

"I love you, too."

When she once again winced in pain, he bent down to

scoop her up into his strong arms, tossing the suitcase and his coat carelessly onto the floor.

"We'd better get out of here before this baby is born, because there's no way I'm going to deliver him or her." His face and tone were so serious that she couldn't contain another outbreak of hysterical laughter.

"Let's go have our baby," she agreed between chuckles.

"I'm with you." He smiled before nearly running out of the door with his panting, giggling wife.

* * * * *

REQUEST YOUR FREE BOOKS!

2 FREE NOVELS PLUS 2 FREE GIFTS!

KIMANI™ ROMANCE

Love's ultimate destination!

KROM11B